November Starfall

Barbra Badger

November Starfall

Barbra Badger

November Starfall
Copyright 2016

This book is a work of fiction. This story, including names of characters and incidents, are the products of the author's imagination or are used fictitiously. Any resemblance to actual events, public or private institutions, corporations, or persons living or deceased, is purely coincidental.

No part of this publication may be reproduced, stored in a retrieval system, or transmitted in any form or by any means, electronic, mechanical, photocopying, recording or otherwise, without written permission of the author.

ISBN-13: 978-0-9982438-0-1

Printed in the United States of America

DEDICATION

Choosing one person for a dedication can be daunting. However, in this case there is a standout. Adrienne Ellis Reeves, whose first publication appeared when she was seventy years old. She has mentored and supported many budding authors and at ninety, released *Charleston Visions*, her eleventh or twelfth novel. You will be enriched if you read any of her novels, but th3e last is the fruition of her dream.

ACKNOWLEDGMENTS

To Mike Foley for being a teach, editor, and giving encouragement.

To October Writers Group for years of listening and critiquing this and many other efforts in the art of writing.

Also to my husband for adapting to my absences for writing meetings and conferences and providing financial support for my "artful" projects.

To my Native American friends who offered approval of this novel.

To Jenny Margotta for everything!

And last but definitely not least, to the California Writers Club, High Desert Branch for providing sources upon sources of how to do this craft well and who to ask when you don't know.

One

Savannah Georgia Dunbar—Born November 11, 1833

All over the world stars were falling in such numbers that, in the cloudless places, a person could read by them at night. In large cities people were terrified, ran to their churches, hid under the bed and the children stared at the sky until their heavy lids would no longer allow it.

Under the celestial shower, sat a small farmhouse on the Iowa prairie. Julia Dunbar was giving birth in the rough-hewn bed her husband had made. Her sister, Clara, was still a day's travel away. In her absence, an Indian woman from a nearby clan was helping with the birth.

The true father of the child, Blue Stone, was an important man in the local Lakota tribe. Blue Stone was known for being a strong hunter. He had had a powerful vision during his first Sun Dance. He was a kind man who hunted on behalf of widows and elders. He was named for a large, valuable piece of turquoise in his possession. The times and place dictated that any relationship between he and Julia could not exist, beyond the conception of this child. Yet, a bond between them transcended Julia's generations of Catholic teachings and Blue Stones' traditional tribal courting rituals. They remained connected in spirit without any means of communication between them other than that of the heart.

Between her pains Julia paced, then stopped to gaze through the only window in the humble home, at the silent wonder in the sky. And when the pains would allow she stood as long as she could searching the horizon. All the while urging her soul to fly to the true father of this child, to tell him it was on *this* night that his child was being born.

The Indian woman, Many Beads, was of his clan and had been asked to be midwife in Clara's absence. She would share the news with Blue Stone as soon as she returned to the camp.

Phineas Dunbar married Julia knowing she carried an Indian's child. He had heard some women at church saying horrible things about Julia, but when he met her, he immediately fell in love with her.

During her labor, Phineas paced in the barn until he heard the child cry. He promised himself he would raise this child as his own and do everything he could to protect and teach the child, boy or girl. While he waited the many hours in the barn, he even planned the lessons he wanted to share in great detail. *We'll ride in all kinds of weather, hunt game in fall and fish in summer. I will take my child far from our house and show him how always to find his way home. We can build an icehouse to fish in winter, ride, rope ...* His thoughts picked up speed and spun out of control. Finally, he whispered a prayer, "God, give us a strong, healthy child. I will do the rest." He stepped out of the barn and marveled at the display the heavens continued to produce. He felt reassurance from that marvel that his prayer was being answered.

Phineas had stayed with a clan of Indians for a few months as a child. He became lost from the small group of travelers heading to Iowa from Missouri and the family assumed he had died or been taken by the Indians and had no means or fortitude to take him back.

He learned much from them and retained that knowledge. The band he had stayed with found his family and returned him in better health than he was found.

Many Beads was a good midwife in the clan, and when she was chosen to help, she waited until after sundown to go to the Dunbar farm. Attitudes toward the native people in the area were mixed. Ranging from murderous hatred to inter- marrying, it was better if no one saw an Indian woman going to a white person's home. Those who intermarried tended to be men marrying the native woman and then living with her tribe to avoid the backlash against her from the murderous whites.

Many Beads had brought hundreds of Native children into the world and word of her skills spread to the White women through the trading post. A woman from the nearest church visited the Lakota camp to exchange goods and ask Many Beads to help Julia whenever the labor began. That day Phineas rode to the camp and called for her to come.

As soon as the mid wife left the village, Blue Stone went to the sweat lodge to purify his body, mind, and spirit to be able to accept another man raising the child of his seed. He sought the spirits to give strength to his child, give it powers to survive and be strong of heart. The visions given him during the *inipi* were reassuring to him, as well. He went in hopeful and one full day later came out very humble.

The spirits told him the child was a girl and showed her riding and hunting. These were not the ways of his people, but her existence did not reflect those ways. At the end of his vision, he saw her wearing a white doeskin dress and carrying a hawk on her arm. Over her left eye a wide swath of snow-white hair gleamed.

When he emerged from the sweat lodge in the evening, the falling stars were thick as swarming bees, yet another promise of a good life for his child.

Unknown to Blue Stone, his uncle, Medicine Bear had already seen this child in a vision of his own. When Blue Stone was a young boy, Medicine Bear went on his name changing vision quest. It ended by Medicine Bear seeing the end of his own life and the beginning of this child's. He couldn't know it at the time, but the mysterious red-haired woman in his vision and the baby in her arms were destined to be in his nephew's future. Only when Blue Stone confided in him the child about to be birthed was his own, was it clear what the meaning of that part of his vision could be.

Julia's sister, Clara, arrived the day after the baby was born. But being November and the first snows freezing water sources, she knew her sister would need her help caring for the newborn and helping Julia heal.

She lived in Midlothian, Illinois near the Mississippi River and often saw the southern ladies in a nearby town. The paddlewheel boats would let them shop while the boat picked up cargo and passengers.   *sweat lodge

Clara watched the graceful women stroll the boardwalk in their beautiful bell-like gowns, hats and parasols. She thought they

3

looked like giant flowers from a garden tended by a master. Sometimes she would strike up a conversation with them.

"Hollyhocks or Morning Glories with the parasols being buds," she thought.

"Where might you be traveling from?" She could guess correctly, but loved the company of these genteel creatures.

"Savannah," or "New Orleans", or "Baton Rouge," they would respond in their soft Southern drawl, exuding politeness and then make comments on the friendliness of the locals or the unique shops. The boats engine would be breathing in the background and spewing huge plumes of steam, adding drama to every word.

Clara told Julia about the ladies and their beautiful gowns. "And they have such lovely hands, and wear the sweetest perfume. Most of them are from Savannah Georgia..."

The words faded as Julia heard the musical sound in that name—Savannah, Georgia. It rolled off the tongue gracefully, grace that she wanted her child to know. The reality of their lives, however, was far from the wishes she held for her daughter.

Several miles away, a young boy, Webster Michaels, ten years old, was watching the same starfall. Webster Michaels had met Blue Stone, who had stopped and cared for him when he had been thrown from his horse, knocking the wind out of him. That moment forged a friendship that neither of them could have imagined.

Savannah was born at 11 minutes past 11:00 pm on the 11th of November 1833. Her skin was dark brown at birth. Julia knew in an instant her hopes for an easy life for this child wouldn't be realized, but kept the name, hoping it would smooth her path anyway. When Phineas saw the baby was a girl his heart melted and he vowed to teach her all he would have if she were a boy. He wanted this child to be able to survive no matter what.

Many Beads took the news to Blue Stone. "The child is a girl—she looks Lakota, and has our skin color. Do you want me to steal her and bring her to you?"

Fire flashed through Blue Stone's eyes, eyes that usually reflected tenderness.

"Leave this clan. Go to your relations to the north and stay until spring," he roared. The whole clan was surprised by his reaction and helped Many Beads to scurry away.

He felt badly for his gruffness and asked Medicine Bear to have his guardians protect her.

Medicine Bear had been given the gift of being able to talk to animals and understand them and heal them with special herbs and dances. He rarely used these gifts for the benefit of humans, but being blood relative to Blue Stone he agreed to do it.

There were a batch of crows and a small group of coyotes that he sent to follow Many Beads and to come tell him if there were any problems. The coyotes would handle predators and the crows could cover ground by flying over obstacles and rivers to keep watch. They could also mob any creature by diving and pecking at them.

Two

Savannah—1849—Sixteen Years Old

"Sa-van-nah!" Those three syllables ripped through the air as long, high pitched shrieks, carrying urgency and pain across the distance. Her mother, Julia, had just received the news that her husband, Phineas, was dead. Savannah gathered up her many underskirts and ran full bore to her mother's side. Wings seemed to carry her bare feet as they slapped against the rocky patches, sank into the mud mixed with manure and, finally, landed her onto the porch steps and took her to her mother's side.

Her father, Phineas, had been missing for more than a year. Savannah was resigned to the idea of his death, but Julia had to hold on to hope.

The man who had come to tell Julia about Phineas' death was from the next county. Savannah remembered him from the harvestings or barn raisings when folks came from miles around to help.

As Savannah ran onto the porch, she heard him talking to her mother. "Missus, I can send my boys over to help out for a while. And my wife, too, if you like. But as for me, I have …" He turned the brim of his hat 'round in his fingers and looked at the floor as he spoke. Savannah noticed a line where his hat usually rested between his leathery, skinned face and the starkly pale forehead creased with sincere concern.

"Thank you, but our nearest neighbors, just east of us, can come, and my husband's brother, Orville, is only twelve miles to the northeast." Julia graciously replied.

Her father's wake took place a week later. The coffin was filled with lye and remained closed: the moldering mass inside wouldn't be recognized by anyone who loved him. This was the first barrier that

6

had ever existed between Savannah and her father, other than the time and distance that kept them apart when he rode off that day in late February.

It was April of 1849 and Savannah was sixteen. Although she had lived on this farm all her life, she had never seen most of the people in her house today. Savannah picked up pieces of conversations as she circled the room.

"... neighbor had gone to identify the body."

"... everyone felt it would be too great a shock for Julia."

"Phineas had been 'crushed under his horse"... and

"... been dead a long while before anyone found them."

Savannah kept her little brother, Sean, from tripping guests as he crept about on the floor. This tiny cabin, which until today had seemed roomy, now felt like the suits the men were wearing—a few sizes too small. The cedar absorbed by the women's dresses competed with the food smells and made the air (almost thick enough to swallow), close in.

Mrs. Gibson had the best dress, deep maroon velvet, festooned in lace with a cameo the size of a plum. It stood out in the crowd, most of whom had only covered buttons to boast. Mrs. Gibson's daughter helped to look after Sean creeping about the floor. Julia's dark green taffeta emphasized her golden red locks. Her beauty was in her skin, eyes and hair. These were the things that had made the women jealous. They all kept their distance once they expressed their sympathy.

The aromas that mingled from the table were maples, apples (sent from relatives in northeast), spices (a real find, rarely available at the trading post), mustards, hams, and roasted chickens giving up their savory scents.

Guided by Savannah and the Gibson's daughter, Sean finally found a safe place under the table laden with the collage of food. Keeping her eyes on Sean gave her an excuse not to return the querying—even judgmental—gazes and slanted scowls of the guests. She knew she was much darker than any other member of her small family and anyone else in the room—a fact that had always raised eyebrows and elicited snide remarks from neighbors, they carelessly expressed.

Even though she spent most of her days outside doing chores, it didn't account for the overall deep shade of her skin. She had a tinge of auburn in her hair—from her Irish mother—but no other attributes matched family traits. Her brother had their mother's milk-white skin and Phineas' wide shoulders and gray eyes. Even at fourteen months he looked like he belonged, but Savannah didn't. The broad white streak in her hair over her left eye also set her apart from any other person she had ever seen--yet another distinct reason to be seen as 'different'.

Savannah often felt that she had come from a distant land—or sprouted up from the ground—instead of being born into this family. In summer, she just turned darker. Her mother turned painfully pink, in spite of the enormous bonnet she wore. The back of her father's neck peeled all summer, but neither had skin that turned browner and browner, like Savannah's, as the summer months passed.

Iowa sun could be as brutal as the winds in winter. Savannah embraced the extremes of heat and cold. She turned her face into the wind and felt a holy connection when her bare feet were touching the earth in spring and summer.

Mid-afternoon of the wake the preacher rode up on a workhorse he'd had to borrow. Savannah grinned when she saw him awkwardly perched on that massive beast. The man was short. His stumpy legs stuck straight out into the air, and his body bobbed up and down as the "ol' fur-hoofed mound of a horse"—as the preacher referred to him—trundled up to the house. She held the reins while he slithered down the side of the beast, ignoring Savannah, and headed straight for Julia.

"Missus Dunbar," he said.

Savannah had to think a minute. She rarely heard her mother called Mrs. Dunbar. The odd little man continued.

"My sinceeeerest condolences, my dear. How are the children taking it? Been reading your Bible daily? How is your health? Haven't seen you at church for a while. Perhaps this will inspire you to attend more often."

Savannah noticed that he didn't take a breath or seem to

care if Julia answered or not. She surveyed the rest of the visitors and noticed most of them tried not to notice her. The one exception was her Aunt Clara, who had always treated Savannah like family.

Clara and her husband had come as soon as they received word about Phineas' death. Clara was truly sad for Julia—they were sisters after all—but Clara's husband, Harley, stayed out by the barn, rolling and smoking tobacco, and shirking from any contact with Julia, Sean or Savannah.

Now Clara sought Savannah out and found the girl near the table. "Did you get the journal I sent?" she asked. "I wasn't sure if it would get here for your birthday, but that was my intention." Whenever Clara spoke to her, Savannah noticed the same kindness as when she spoke to Julia. Unlike most of the women at the church, who were condescending, hateful or pitying, if they spoke to Savannah at all.

"Yes. Thank you," Savannah replied. "It came to the trading post a few days after my birthday—bad weather. It was just in time. The last one you sent was filled up. Thank you," she said as she backed out of the door.

Savannah wanted to be away from the closeness of the room and headed out to the barn. Uncle Harley was still there at the far end, staying as far from any other people as possible. How he and Clara ever got married was a mystery to the girl.

Harley always glared at Savannah whenever they were together. He was rude and cold to Julia, and hung his head around Phineas. Even little Sean, a boy child, got no recognition from him. Savannah had felt it was just Harley's way until now. Today she read more into his demeanor. His outright rejection and abhorrence of her was clear, and his coldness hurt. Beyond being shy, disgust radiated from him, and she concluded it always had. Those who spurned her, even family, were the ones who should feel shame, not her, she decided.

Her father had given her comfort naturally and freely. She ached for the strength of 'Father' to be near, but her stoicism made it impossible to show.

The barn smells of hay, manure, and the soft muttering of her horse Huck were all comforting to her. Peering over an empty stall, she watched the new batch of kittens mewing in the corner. The mother had gone hunting, and they were exposed to danger and powerless. Their eyes were still sealed shut; they were creeping about on quivering miniature limbs, boldly expressing their fear in every cry.

She felt that vulnerable herself, but now her mother and baby brother needed her to be like the mother cat, in spite of her own need for comfort. Harley wasn't around much, and didn't really help when he was. Harley's brother, Orville, who lived much closer to the Dunbar's, made an effort to help as much as he could. Even after Phineas disappeared, he continued to help Julia and Savannah as time allowed.

After the preacher said his words in the early evening, Julia comforted herself by holding Sean, the one warm body in the house that she could physically cling to. Petting his curls and smelling his skin and hair helped her to relax; it showed on her face. Since no one was paying any attention to her—as usual—Savannah was free to mingle and taste the various dishes.

A girl about ten, Chordillia Philpott, with skin the color of Julia's, waggled back and forth as she stood next to Savannah while dipping a finger into every dish. She licked her finger after each taste then put it back into the next bowl. Her ringlets were tied back with a pink satin ribbon and her skin looked like it never saw the sun. She had a menacing look on her face, but nothing else about her demeanor seemed threatening.

"Why did your mother name you Savannah Georgia? That's a very odd name. Isn't that a town somewhere?" Chordillia said, almost purring and feigning friendliness. She tilted her head and squinted one eye, her posture forthright, privileged, expecting an answer.

"She's hoping I can go there some day and thought naming me that might help." She answered with her own forthrightness, tinted with defiance. "Mother says all the women wear beautiful dresses and have lots of servants there, so they don't wear out their hands," This was far more information than she was really willing to give and she waited for a response. When none was offered she bluntly asked,

"What's your name?"

"My name is Mathilda Cordelia Philpot. I don't think there is a town named after me."

I sincerely hope to heaven there's not, thought Savannah.

"Are you related to me?" the girl followed up with bold-faced sarcasm. Savannah gritted her teeth and blotted out the thought as she spoke it aloud. She knew father would be proud of her restraint.

"No. I don't think so, anyway," she said.

"My father found your ... father. He was already quite dead, you know." Now she looked straight at Savannah. "Why are you so dark, father said the man he found was a white man? How did you get so dark are you a ..."

Savannah knew the rest of the question and interrupted the query. "I thank him for telling someone. Thank him again for all of us," she said as she twirled away out the door. The way the sun was lighting the orchard was irresistible and she could no longer bear to remain indoors.

When she was sure no one was looking, she snuck back in, secreted her journal under her arm, and went back outside to read it, slowly. Memories on those pages were her only comfort. Mother needed to cling to Sean; Clara was looking after Mother. Savannah's nature meant she was never sitting in any one place for long. She hid her precious book in the folds of her skirt as she walked from a tree to the barn to the orchard to spend time with memories of her father in those precious pages. She could hear his words now, whispered in her memories. "You're a very special girl with a blessed destiny for your life."

She always felt his words were more than a wish or even parental pride. *What did he know?*, she thought, *When would he tell her why he thought that way?* There were so many questions for him that would never be answered. Today the most glaring one was, "Why am I **so** different?"--she shouted aloud.

Leaning against the apple tree, and hidden by the overburdened branches, she read:

May 14th, 1843: Dear Diary, Father is teaching
me how to shoot. He wants me to hunt rabbits while he
is plowing, planting, and minding the animals. The first

time I fired the rifle, myself, I fell backwards so hard it knocked the wind out of me. Father is so strong! How can he just stand there and not move when he shoots? We laughed when I got up, because my legs had gone straight up in the air. I must have looked like a turtle on its back. He brushed the dust off me and gave me a big hug. He promised we will try again in a few months, when I am stronger. He said, "I know you can become strong, strong in body and in spirit."

She caressed the pages and passages about her father and skipped over those few with no mention of him.

Moving to the back side of the barn, facing the setting sun, she read:

July 5th, 1843: Dear Diary, Mother went to town and will stay overnight at Orville's. It's too far to go to Fish Fork and come back the same day. Father and I did all the chores and then we played with the new foal. She has a tiny, squeaky voice and the longest legs on any animal I have ever seen. Father explained that the foal came out of her mother after the stallion 'lay on her back'. I thought he was attacking her. Father picked me up and carried me back to the house while he told me about the horses.

I was ten and that will be seven years ago in July, she recalled ... and read on:

We ate strawberries with cream, played horseshoes and had a wonderful day.

Her face glowed from the sun's last light and she found the last entry that spoke about her father:

March 10th, 1848: Mother says I became a woman today. Father went to find some men to help plow this year. He says his hands are getting too stiff to hold the plow for the whole twenty-five acres.

Even as she read the words she recalled: *I looked at his hands with their broad, graceful fingers. The fingers lay on each other smoothly, but the black stains and callused palms were proof of the endless toil he put forth for our survival.*

Three

Confronting the Hounds of Hell

The preacher was the last to leave the wake. Savannah saw him as a strange little man who always filled his own plate to overflowing. On one visit, she watched him scrape the bowl before mother had served herself, leaving her without a portion. *How can he hold that much? And didn't he notice Mother has no food on her plate? What about the loaves and fishes—everyone got a serving?* Savannah gave her mother half of hers, and then and there closed her mind to the preacher and everything he said in his sermons.

This night Savannah stayed in the shadows as Julia and the preacher sat near the stove—the potbelly stove for which father had traded his beloved pocket watch.

"Missus, I can't say it enough, the children must be given The Word, or they will become a bane to you and be condemned to hell for eternity. Your man, Phineas, awaits you and his child in heaven. I beg you, do not disappoint him."

Her reply was quiet but strong and pointed. "We have a Bible and read it as often as we can. Both of my children know the Lord, sir. As for my man, you can believe he's in heaven, yet he has been speaking to my heart as clearly as if he were standing by my side—all day—every day since he left this house months ago." Julia's gaze never wavered.

The minister countered, "Your state of worry and grief puts those pagan thoughts in your head." Dismissing her mother's heartfelt belief, he went on, "You and the children are sheep that need a shepherd and that is *my* appointed duty. Besides, your oldest—as everyone knows—is of heathen blood and in great need of soul saving. At least insure her entrance into heaven. No man, no decent man," he was hissing now, "will have her for a wife; she will burden you until your own death."

14

Clack-clack.

Savannah readied the rifle but held it with the barrel pointed to the floor. The sound spoke loudly of her intention. Mother looked up, horrified at first, then a smile graced her face like a cloud gently passing over the sun.

Preacher Man was jabbering as he stood up without bending, as though he had just sat upon a tack. "You see! That's just what I mean. This, this … aboriginal aberration will bring you nothing but trouble and is headed straight for the hounds of hell."

Savannah calmly lifted the rifle barrel to rest in the crook of her elbow. Preacher Man headed for the door with his eyes glued on the barrel of the rifle. It followed him. She pointed it at his backside where, if it did go off, would not keep him from his livelihood of ministering to his 'sheep'.

Savannah was filled with gratitude, in that moment and the many moments after she spent reminiscing that she had been taught to ride, rope, and use a rifle. Her legacy from the man she called father was the skill and knowledge to survive in many ways. He had taught her how to make a shelter of snow; how to fish—even through ice— skin the prey and how to medicate lame horses and sick cows. These skills he had learned from his time with the Indians. At the end of this very long day, she wrote:

April 20th, 1849: Dear Diary, Father's wake was today. Tomorrow Orville will come and we will put father in the ground. Preacher seems to think my soul is doomed to keep company with the 'hounds of hell'. I prefer their company to his.

She remembered the time Phineas had asked her why she disliked going to church. She had answered emphatically, "I don't believe that getting all wet, and having an impolite man tell you that you are 'saved', gets you a place in heaven. I have felt warm, wanted, weak and loved all at once, many times—Mother calls it being in awe and humble—or a spiritual experience but I have never felt it in that church."

The compassion on Phineas' face told her he understood her every word. She continued gazing at the sky and speaking as though he wasn't there, "It happens when I'm outside or riding Huck. It always comes with the knowing I am a small thing in a great creation, feeling a part of everything I see and whatever it is that gives me the warm, wanted, weak feeling. If that makes me 'saved', then I am. If it doesn't, I don't care and don't want to be, and when I die I'll be happy to join the hounds of hell he talks about."

Several weeks after the wake, Savannah found the courage to ask Julia. "Who is my real father? And does he have anything to do with why you would stand at the fence and search the horizon in all kinds of weather when Phineas was away?"

Julia, picking cucumbers in the garden, froze in mid-bend. A flicker of relief passed through her expression. Her shoulders suddenly relaxed, as though she had been waiting for this day to come. She took her daughter's hand and drew her to sit close beside her.

They sat in the garden, oblivious to the bees landing on their shoulders or how the damp earth was clinging to their skirts. Her voice softened to a near whisper. Savannah listened as Julia explained. "When I was eighteen I fell from a wagon. My head hit a rock."

She told how Blue Stone had found her, took her to a nearby stream, built a shelter using his robe, shirt, and horse blanket over willow branches. She told how he cared for her with herbs and teas for several days. "When I woke, he was still near me. His eyes were deep and kind. I was not at all afraid." Julia must have held a vision of those eyes in her mind as she spoke. "His hair was gleaming white even though he was young—and his hands were so masculine and yet gracefully sculpted ..." Her voice trailed, as the imprint of him tenderly touching her face as his eyes expressed his love for her. "His name was Blue Stone," she continued. "He was a Sioux. I am not sure is he is still alive," her voice nearly faded completely, "I told Clara with the only words I could find about something wordless. What happened between us I could never explain to anyone. We didn't speak the same language—at least not in words—but we felt like we were the only people in the world and being together was all that mattered. It was something beyond our control—in the hands of destiny."

Savannah had no reference for such an experience and couldn't even begin to understand. For an instant she wanted to ask her mother about her own destiny, the one that Phineas had often referred to, but that thought was quickly overshadowed by other thoughts.

Why hasn't Mother ever told me before? How could she keep this from me? What am I to think of this Indian, who obviously took advantage of my mother's weakness and ignorance? If I ever meet him, I will have his scalp!

Julia continued, "Phineas Dunbar married me, knowing I carried Blue Stone's child. And he raised you as surely as if you were his. He helped you grow courageous, curious, honest and independent. Even the temper that riles under your hat didn't discourage him from being patient with you. He let you be whatever urgings might run through your veins command you to be."

Savannah felt the strength of those urgings to breathe, to run, to ride just for the joy of it all. Every season she drank in the essences and tested herself against the extremes. But she was not ready to be grateful to the Indian whose ink had colored her entire existence, and caused others to look at her in shame and distrust to this very day. *Regardless of how he may have deceived Julia*, she thought. Savannah couldn't allow herself to even think of Blue Stone as her father.

Walking back to the house hand in hand, Savannah saw her mother step lighter, breathe easier, and smile with her eyes and her lips. Her mother being unburdened from the secret released a measure of inner beauty Savannah had never seen before.

Savannah believed in her heart that her real 'father' had an evil intent, someone who should be punished. Nevertheless, she resolved that those thoughts would remain hidden from Julia. She released Julia's hand absorbed with the peace on her mother's face. Her eyes reflected gratitude for Julia, but her stomach roiled with anger. Wood took the punishment to dispel the rage she felt. If she allowed it, that rage would burn the accursed dark brown skin off her bones. Each log was a limb being severed from the evil-spirited Indian.

Two years later, four days after her eighteenth birthday, the hounds of hell came to the farm. Masked riders thundered in and brought death with them. Their hatred for Indians—and rumors of an Indian massacre—spurred them to the Dunbar farm where 'one of them' lived. They started in the barn, killed all the livestock, then rode past the henhouse and set it on fire.

With thundering hooves, clattering and crashing of breaking porcelain and glass, one rider reared his horse to break down the front door. Before Savannah could reach her rifle, he shot Julia and little Sean. They lay inches apart, their blood mingling on the floor. Sean was gone instantly; Julia reached for him but only touched a lock of his hair as she sighed her last breath.

By now the girl had grabbed her rifle—and discovered it empty. She kept it empty in the house for the safety of Sean who had found it once, loaded.

The leader riled up his horse and charged at her to intimidate her as she stood in the blood of her mother pooling at her feet with her empty rifle.

Savannah stood staunch before the frothing horse in the dismantled doorframe and stared up at the demon holding the gun that had just killed her family. The demon spoke through the flour sack that covered all but its eyes.

The thin cloth flapped like discarded snakeskin with every movement of his foul breath. "Now you know how the Jensen daughter feels. Your *real* kin kilt all her kin, and you know what kin I'm talking about. Stole all the livestock and raided the smokehouse. The Gibsons tuk her in, but just see if anyone takes you in. No! By God, over our dead bodies—no one will take *you* in."

When he rode across the expanse of the property, it took all of Savannah's strength not to load the gun and shoot him in the back.

The voice and what she had seen of the eyes were familiar. She was sure he was one of the 'elders' in Preacher Man's church. One of those people with hearts colder than January night winds, who secreted their hate behind false smiles. One of those people she never felt a part of or wanted to be.

His words were prophetic. No one did come: not Mr. Philpot, the man from the next county who had told the authorities about father, not the closest neighbor, not even her father's brother, Orville. Her deepest fear was a reality. She didn't belong to this family, these people. She wasn't one of the 'sheep' in that church. Now she had no home, no family, no God—and for now, no time for grieving.

Four

Surviving

Necessity forced her to enter the burning house, for what she wasn't sure, but boots, bullets, a blanket and her journal were the only treasures she came out with. A November night was not the time to be in a nightgown so she wrapped some clothes into the blanket and got as far into the yard as the fence, when the roof came crashing down.

The base of the big oak provided the pallet for her rest. Deep sleep came upon her and she didn't move a muscle until dawn.

Loneliness began to color her thoughts in brief moments. Searching for useful items in the ashes, a dainty piece of lace from Julia's dress, or a glimpse of Sean's quilt, brought burning tears to her eyes and a peach-sized lump to her throat. Swiftly changing her gaze she noticed providence had caused the roof to collapse in a single piece covering the bodies and only smoke had seeped under it, leaving the bodies unscathed by flames. But she couldn't lift the piece to know and was grateful that they were at least covered and protected.

She fought off her grief by planning for survival. There were times no amount of denial would suffice and tears from out of nowhere streamed down her cheeks. Unaware of the emotion behind them, she kept sorting through the rubble for the basic needs for her survival. A thought of Blue Stone usually stopped the tears and she could think again of survival.

There were plenty of provisions in the woods a quarter mile from the house. The stream, edible plants and, if needed, rabbits, squirrels and birds. She set up a lean-to near the oak and prepared to live there for a time to figure out the rest of her plans. *I'll collect whatever I can from the ashes of our house to trade with. And I've got to find my journals,* she thought.

The next day while organizing the camp, she was startled by the sound of a horse, but his whinny assured her he was a friend. A familiar muzzle parted the shrubs, "Huck! How did you escape the fire? How did you find me? You fine friend." He tenderly caressed one arm as she hugged his neck with the other. His familiar scent was tinged with charred fur and much of his mane was burnt off. She combed the melted hairs with her fingers and cleaned the ash and grit from his wounds with a velvet touch and whispers of compassion.

"Huck, we have some traveling to do." She almost sang the words. Providence was finally favoring her. She had already salvaged the saddle and bridle. Even without a horse, something had told her to take them as she passed the shed where they had been protected. No horses survived the barn fire.

Her journal, spare clothes, some jerky, a few flints, father's good knife and some small bags of flour and sugar and a canteen didn't weigh Huck down. His muscles rippled and he ruffed frequently in harmony with the urgency Savannah expressed with her actions. She wanted to get word to Clara as soon as possible. Tearing a page from the journal she wrote a quick note and folding it, sealing it with pine sap she waited for an opportunity to send it off.

Not long after, a stagecoach rumbled up behind her. As she distracted the driver, she slipped the note to Clara into the mailbag. It simply said, 'Mother and Sean have been killed. House and barn burned down. Don't come here. Too dangerous. I will find you.'

Clara loved getting mail and would hold each letter to her heart before opening it. This one was very sticky with the pine sap and she didn't recognize the handwriting, but she did recognize the paper from the journal she had sent her niece.

These odd circumstances gave her a sense of foreboding. Walking slowly into the house, not wanting to open it at all, she felt her heart sink even before she read it.

As she read the letter to Harley, he just kept nodding. Clara was weeping uncontrollably and rocking back and forth, repeating,

"Julia, Julia, and that sweet baby."

Harley was nonchalant. "Phineas asked for all this tragedy when he married your sister. He knew she was carrying an Indian half-breed child. I don't know how he could stand to look at that woman or that half-breed once it was born. If you hadn't gone there for the birthing and helped, it might have froze to death, and all this trouble wouldn't have happened at all."

There had been few suitors in the far reaches of the plains where Clara's father had settled. He resolved Harley 'would do' for the reason that the man owned the most property and seemed to have a knack for business that didn't include farming. Father paid no mind to Clara's wishes or to the small mindedness and quick temper of the man. The times and circumstance dictated the fate of most settlers and farmers, more so the women. She obeyed her father's wishes.

But now, Clara could be still no longer. "Harley, you are a hard-working man, and I appreciate this home and all that you provide for me. But I will not abide your hateful words any more. I don't expect you to change your mind but don't speak those venomous words in this house or I swear I will find somewhere else to live. My sister and her baby have been killed. Have you no pity whatsoever? Her daughter has no home and is alone in the world now. I have known your feelings about her but, if she chooses us to help her—*I will find a way!*"

Harley had never heard his wife speak that way or in that tone, to anyone and certainly not him. He took his wounded pride and disappeared for hours, while Clara began to plan how she might help her niece.

Furniture in the parlor could be placed in the dining room, and a bed put in its place. She had seen a nice dresser at the Jordan's and the missus said, "It's just in the way. I have no use for it, but there is nowhere else to put it." Clara made a note to ask her about it at church. A wash bowl, a few lamps, a small rug near the bed for cold mornings, and it would be perfect for her guest.

Clara recalled the last time she had seen Savannah. A white streak had begun to stand out in Savannah's pure black hair. That streak stood out starkly just over her right eye, two inches wide and as pure white as new snow. Julia had said her "Indian" had snow-white hair even in his young years. The rest of Savannah's hair was thick and rich black with a mere suggestion of red. Her glossy hair and strong features were a statement to her Sioux ancestry.

Clara wept for the loss of Julia and Sean while fervently hoping Savannah would somehow find her way in the world.

"Dear God," she prayed aloud, "bring me that child and keep her safe in her travel."

Simultaneously, Savannah was using all that Phineas taught her, added to all that her own genes knew from instinct, to get to Clara.

The only thing Savannah knew about being Lakota was that it was a cause for hatred, hatred so strong it overcame all sense of humanity. She bore her own hatred for that ancestry every day, but this day she rode off to catch the steamboat that could take her to Clara's.

"There's nothing I can do about any of this, Huck," Savannah whispered to her horse. "There's no reason for me to stay here. I'm gonna find Blue Stone, no matter how long or far I have to go. Don't know yet what I'll do when I find him, but first, to Clara's. Let's go, Huck."

Savannah had never been farther than the nearest town of Lynn Grove. Clara lived in Illinois across the Mississippi, that's all she knew about the world she now faced, this world intent on giving her pain.

But for now, Huck's arrival lifted her spirits and she rode with the wind caressing her face; the forward momentum made her feel something she had never experienced before and which could only be called 'glorious freedom'.

Medicine Bear spent a whole day in the sweat lodge. He called upon many animals to keep the girl safe. After doing the smudging and sending the pungent sage smoke in every direction, it rose out of his teepee with the message to the animals and drifted far beyond the land that he knew.

23

———————————

Three braves lay in the tall grass, unseen—watching her joy as Savannah rode.

Five

Time to grieve—Time to Grow

Her first meal that wasn't jerky was pheasant. She had stopped to rest her bones and saw a female gathering nest material across the expanse. Watching for hours, until the bird no longer left the grassy area it was working in, she tip-toed up and grabbed it by the neck in a lightning quick move. Phineas had shown her that the males keep several females and that meant the birds would continue to produce.

The moment the bird's life force left it, she said, "Thank you for your life and the life you are about to give me." It felt natural, so completely that she continued to do that for the rest of her own life. She thanked all the animal life she consumed.

After a few days of riding, she came upon some fellow travelers. She gave them some flour and sugar and a few trinkets she had saved from the house to use for exchange and got two pairs of trousers, a shirt, and a poncho. She strapped on her father's side arm; the belt held up the trousers, the poncho hid her female form and she rode unmolested to find a steamboat that would take her to Aunt Clara's side of the river.

Father had taught her that the sun moves from east to west, to gauge time by its movement and, generally, use its position for direction. However, it was April, and for days the sky remained gray from first light until night. The initial rush of joy at being free had worn off and being outside in the cold breath of encroaching winter, with only her plodding horse for company, gave her reason and room to grieve.

The grayness of the days engulfed her and eventually weighed down through her. Her arms and legs felt like lead, her neck gave up holding her heavy head and all she could see was Huck's hoof plodding through sod. In a wide meadow, she let out a shattering wail. The croak of a startled crow echoed through the trees, the snap of twigs, and crunch of the leaves under the steed's hooves gave sound to her breaking heart.

The other crows lifted off en masse, carrying the sting of her agony heavenward and beyond the limits of her sight. After releasing that pain, she wrote in her diary:

I grieve for my family, their home—not really for myself. I am more content out here—in the wild. My soul is at peace. Bird songs quiet me, the smells of decaying leaves, the silt-laden river, and the awareness of day moving toward night stir something inside. I don't know how to find Clara—but I know I will. I feel all my senses coming alive. I smell game and water; my eyes see clues for tracking, I understand the meanings of birdcalls and their silence. I will find Clara and then Blue Stone. If it takes the rest of my life, I will find Blue Stone—I know I will.

In the forest, Indian braves followed, unseen, behind her.

Six

New Territory

After two more days, the air was thick with the moisture and the odor of the nearby river blocked out all other scents. The Mississippi was a day away, but its encompassing power touched everything. Water lines twelve feet up on the trees marked the height from the last flooding. Stories of that mighty vein made it difficult to sort tall tales from reality. Her progress was painful and slow. She grunted through a mulch of birch leaves a foot deep, rotting, mildewing, and melting into the mud below. It sucked strength from Huck. He struggled valiantly through the mass, each step burying his legs up to his knees. Images of her father trapped under his maimed horse kept popping into her head.

"We gotta get out of this mess," she blurted. The horse nodded vigorously. She stood still calf deep in the mud, stroking his mane; then … in the forest … rapid hoof beats.

Those guys are on solid ground!

She turned in time to see the braves riding through the forest as though there wasn't a tree in sight. Before she could put her hand on her sidearm, they were already out of range and out of view although she could still hear the hoof beats.

"I guess they know something I don't. Let's go." Savannah tugged at a ninety-degree angle and the horse followed. They hit solid ground in fifty yards.

She couldn't trust the Indians. Although she was aware that she was kin to those braves, she didn't know the truth about their culture or humanity. Fear imprinted by people more willing to hate than to understand formed her own reactions. *For all I know that damned red-skin Blue Stone forced himself on my mother. That story she told was made up. Maybe she even believed it. I don't. Did he force you? Did he, Mother? Is that the truth?*

She expected an answer and it came. Memories emerged of her mother standing out by the far fence, staring into the infinite horizon in all kinds of weather. One by one, her memories drifted past her mind's eye. For many years and in every season, whenever Father was away, Julia had stood at the fence at sundown.

Savannah remembered when she was about eight years old; she stood beside her mother one January at dusk. A wind blew fresh snow in their faces. In spite of being wrapped in a heavy blanket, Julia shivered from head to toe. Savannah wrapped herself inside the blanket to add warmth to her mother. Tears trickling down Julia's face froze halfway down. She looked down and read the compassion in Savannah's eyes and never let her attend any future reveries. Her daughter was beginning to be aware enough to ask questions that Julia was not ready to answer.

Reflecting on those times, Savannah conceded that her mother had loved the Indian. The thought was incongruous with anything else she knew of the 'heathens'. But that look could not be understood any other way. Julia must have loved the Indian.

"How *could* you love someone who forced himself on you?" pushing the words out released the knot in her stomach. The memory burned away with a flare of anger. Her assumption would not be challenged. There had never been any example or story in her life about Indians that made them seem human. In this moment she fancied herself to be the only one. Daydreaming was over.

Settlements sprouted along the river, their presence best detected at night, when lanterns, campfires, and the flash of hunters' gunfire in early evening forged through the thick forestland. Thoughts of those homey, warm cabins reminded her of what she wanted most. "Huck, I sure would like a bath, but the river is no place to do that. I notice you don't drink from there much."

Sleep brought dreams of having a bath, being wrapped in a clean towel, and snuggling in a feather blanket. Waking in the morning, she was spurred on to Clara's. After two hours of riding the river was finally in sight.

Seeing the river was one thing, finding a reliable means to cross it proved to be much more of a challenge. Following its path for miles, she saw a wide clearing, a small hut, and a barge with several horses and men with satchels gathered around waiting to board it. She stayed out of sight and watched it cross two times.

When an Indian, dressed in white man's clothes, approached and boarded with no trouble, she came out of hiding. From the distance, it seemed the Indian had been accepted, if not welcomed.

What are my chances? A stranger, a woman in a man's clothes, 'a half-breed'. "Let's go Huck, we'll just act like we belong here." Huck galloped up to the raft and she hopped off confidently.

"Gotta get across the Mississip." She'd heard others say it that way.

"Well, this ain't it, but it will get ya there," said one man.

"Hold on there!" said the man collecting fees. "Pay up, Injun! What? You're a woman? Where's yer man …?" He took a closer look. "Or yer maw? What are you? You Injun or Mex … what?"

Not sure he really wanted an answer; he leapt on to the next question. "Aw, jumpin' jiminy, you got money?"

"How much do I need?"

"Ya need two bits. Ya ain't got that, ya cain't ride."

For an instant, she felt like dropping her head and walking away. Instead, she stood tall and staunch as she had when facing the monster with a flour sack on its head. Her courage emerged out of necessity, and like the trousers, she tried it on and felt very comfortable in it. Looking him in the eye, she said, "Mister, I can pay you when I reach the other side."

"How's that then? You a magi-can? Gonna pull two bits outta my ear?"

All the other men chuckled, spat, and grinned, with all their attention on Savannah.

"Some might think what I do is magic, but it just takes practice. Lots of practice."

The mood changed quickly and the men's minds went straight for the gutter; their sneers and asides made that plain.

Savannah pulled the sidearm from its holster and fired three perfect shots into a knothole on the toll shack.

The men stood slack-jawed, except the Indian, grinning broadly. His teeth gleamed in bright contrast to his dark brown skin. The white men's mental images of 'wild encounters' quickly faded.

One of the men paid for her passage on the spot. She led Huck aboard the barge and tied him to the rail with the others. He whuffed softly as she combed his mane with her fingers.

"It'll be alright, Huck," she said. "We're on an adventure."

Nervous laughter and more humble attitudes prevailed on the floating stage. Two of the men openly expressed admiration for her skill with the gun but declined when she offered more demonstrations.

The Indian kept his own company and sat still as a life-like statue for the whole journey. It occurred to her that maybe he could lead her to Blue Stone, but when the barge docked on the other side, the Indian was swift to disappear. Savannah looked down to untie Huck, and when she looked back the Indian was gone—completely—nowhere in sight. *No chance to track down Blue Stone.* Besides, her desire to visit Clara had a compelling power that wouldn't be ignored. When she mounted her horse she asked, "Which way to a boat to Illinois?"

"East—just go east," voice called from behind her, and she turned Huck east, trusting in a great unknown and her own sense of direction.

Seven

Webster Michaels—Rockwell, Iowa—1826

The sky spun around above him as Webster lay in the tall grasses with the wind knocked out of him. He would be nine in two months and at this moment feared he might not live to see the day. Conscious, but barely, he heard the horse that threw him calmly munching on the luscious greenery around him.

The sound of another horse walking slowly through the grass to where the boy lay, combined with the footsteps of a man, came closer until a silhouette leaned over him. Webster's vision was still fuzzy and the sun, directly overhead, half-blinded him. Nevertheless, he could tell that the man had very long hair. Not like any of the men he had seen in his short years but like the men spoken of by the old-timers who fought and traded with the Indians.

Stories of children being kidnapped by them and never seen or heard from again made his heart to pound like a horse at full run.

The Indian carefully felt Webster's arms and legs, gently squeezing them and looking at the boy's face intently for signs of pain. Seeing none, he lifted each of the small limbs and let them drop back to the ground. Next, he compressed the boy's sides firmly but carefully. *Still no signs of pain*, he thought. When he was convinced there were no broken bones, he picked Webster up and carried him to the shade of a tree and gave him some water.

The Indian's face was strong, and his eyes were very kind. He had gleaming white hair that lay on his shoulders. His face and body did not match the whiteness of his hair. He wore a leather shirt and leggings and beaded moccasins with an eagle design on the top. He had five eagle feathers attached to the top of a braid that lay on top of the rest of his unbraided hair and hung down his back to below his shoulders.

Webster watched this Indian as he moved about with purpose and grace. The Indian stood and looked toward Webster's wayward horse and said, "Bad horse. Shoot it."

Webster's eyes popped wide open and he shouted, "No! My Pa will ..."

The Indian's eyes sparkled and then he grinned at the boy. Suddenly, he put a finger to his lips to signal Webster to be quiet. Webster figured the Indian could hear something coming toward them. In one swift motion the man took the reins of his horse in one hand and swung himself on top of it. Then, tucking his body as close to the horse as he could, he rode off at a tangent to the riders coming in their direction.

Webster learned from that trick. The sun was in their eyes, and they couldn't distinguish who or what was moving past them so far away. Shortly after the Indian rode off, two horses and riders emerged from the woods.

"Pa! You found me," Webster called out.

"Ephraim here saw Red, running riderless, and brought me to ya. Boy! What you been doin' out here so long? Your ma needs you to tend the chickens and other fowl. You know that baby keeps her fretting with its wailing so she'll need help to make us supper." Pa's horse twitched nervously, sensing Pa's urgency.

Ephraim turned his horse, "Gotta get back," he hollered as he rode off.

"Pa, Old Red threw me and I had the wind knocked clear outta me. An Indian came and gave me water and helped me get my senses back."

"Indian ... What'd he look like?"

"He was big and strong and had really long white hair with eagle ..."

"Blue Stone!"

"You know him? He was very kind to me, Pa."

"I know *of* him. Heard he saved a white woman two winters back, took real good care of her, then that fall she had an Injun baby."

Webster knew what that meant without understanding the details, but he was still surprised to hear that. The man he had just spent an hour with seemed very moral.

Pa went on. "He's said to be some kind of Holy Man. They say his hair got that white during a Sun dance when he had a very powerful vision. It wasn't like that before."

"Holy man? What does that mean to Indians, Pa?"

"Not sure. They say he's a healer and supposed to have some kinda magical powers. I dunno, sounds like bunk to me."

"But, Pa, he helped me. He checked all my bones to see if they were broke, even my ribs. He didn't move me until he was sure nothing was broken. He was almost as kind as Mother when she's taking care of me. I think he really is a holy man, just the way he … is … the way he moves and …"

"I don't care, son. He's Injun and got a white woman pregnant. That's just not right! Mixing things up like that. Holy man or not. I don't want him around any of my family. Let's go home to your ma. She really needs your help now. Your chores and some of hers are a'waitin fer ya."

Webster heard more stories about Blue Stone as time went by. Some of the drifters and farmhands that came to harvest each fall told of meteors often falling near Blue Stone's tribe's encampment; it was hard to tell the tall tales from the truth as the tellers of the stories embellished at will.

Webster's favorite was about how he got the name Blue Stone. One night, Abe Thomas sat near the fire as it popped and snapped through the tinder Webster laid down beneath the larger logs. Ma had gone to bed and Abe sat in her rocker, darning up his britches, occasionally catching a strand of his beard in a stitch.

"Boy, anyone ever tell you the story how Blue Stone got his name?" Abe asked.

"Well, I'm not sure. There are lots of different versions going around. What's your version, Abe"?

"I happen to be closer to the truth of it than anyone else possibly could be, son."

He took a breath and looked straight into Webster's eyes. "I was married to a woman from his tribe—God rest her soul—and I was in the camp when he came to the Sun Dance where he got his vision." Webster eased down to the floor with his attention fixed on Abe, enthralled.

"You know a Sun Dance has several aspects to it. Sure, it's a kind of a party, but not like a hoedown or a barn-raising. I mean, it's nice to see 'all your relations' as they say it, and eat and dance for days on end but …"

"Sounds like a party to me."

"Yup, but it ain't really. Those braves that do the Sun Dance ritual are in a lot of pain. They do it as a sacrifice."

"What do you mean pain, Abe? How can you dance all day and be in pain?"

"I'll tell ya, but first ya need to understand the purpose. Each one has in his own mind and heart what his pain is for. Besides the braves sacrificing through pain, everybody else brings their most cherished belongings to give them away."

"You mean their horses and beaded clothing and tools?" Webster asked.

"Everything dear to them. Well, I don't know what his name was before he was called Blue Stone, but somehow he earned possession of the biggest piece of turquoise ever seen. The Injuns rumored about it all the time. Some said he had to drag it around by a big strong horse."

They both laughed.

"Anyhow, the elders poke a sharp pointed peg through each side of each man's chest, like this." He pushed the needle through a two-inch wide catch of cloth.

Webster winced and pinched a swath of skin on his own chest.

"Now those pegs are attached to a thong of leather hitched to a cross bar about ten feet off the ground." Abe stretched his arm toward the ceiling as far as it would go. "Then, when the elders see the man is deep in a trance, they pull the thong and lift the man off the ground, and he hangs there attached by his chest until either the pegs rip all the way through and drop him to the ground or until the elders say the dance is over."

Webster's mouth was agape.

"But I can tell you something really strange happened to Blue Stone right at the end of the Sun Dance the day I was there."

Webster leaned in; Abe was nearly whispering.

"Some people said he and his mother went into a trance at the same time. Then he fell to the ground in three inches of dust. He was dead-to-the-world in the trance and the other dancers were gone to the give-away. And I heard the cry of an eagle so close I coulda reached out and grabbed it."

He reached out with his hand and grasped the air, just as a moth was aiming toward Webster's mouth, still hanging open.

"I was only three teepees from his and the sound of the eagle was coming from there. The next thing I know, Blue Stone's coming out of his teepee but no one saw him go in. He come out walking like in his sleep, covered solid from head to toe with the dust he fell in when the tethers tore through his skin, holding twelve large nuggets of turquoise out in front of him like an offering."

"Twelve? How come there was twelve?"

"Folks think that eagle spirit crushed the big one into smaller stones."

"Did ... did he ... did he give ...?"

"Yessir, at last he gave them stones away in the give-away part of the Sun Dance. He gave one to his nephew, for sure ..."

"Nephew?"

"Funny thing about his family. He has an old uncle that limps 'cuz of a short leg, then along comes this youngster—not a child of the crippled uncle—and he has a short leg. The grandmother named him Hopping Squirrel. Most people figgered Blue Stone did his Sun Dance with that little boy on his heart."

"Anyway, 'bout the stones ... one to his nephew and some to some braves he knew were jealous of him, but he gave all of 'em away by the end of the Sun Dance."

"I know the rest," Webster added, "his hair turned all white."

"Yeah, but here's another strange twist to this whole story," Abe said. "Guess where those stones are now."

Webster looked stunned, then puzzled. He tilted his head to one side and asked, "What do you mean? He gave them away; even I

35

know he can't take them back. Indians don't do that. Who should have them?"

"Yup, he gave them away just like everything else he owned. His aunt made him many beautiful breastplates and beaded shirts and moccasins and he always gave them away."

"I saw those moccasins, looked like a lot of work went into those."

"All that would be fine, except he had no offspring to give any of it to, that's why he kept giving it all at the give-aways. He gave his nephew a lot of things almost as soon as his aunt gave them to him."

"So I don't understand? Why is that strange?"

"I'm getting to that, just hold on. The uncle, Medicine Bear, had a vision and he told Blue Stone, 'Give the twelve stones to your daughter from the red-haired woman.' Now, the only person of the tribe that knew about it was Many Beads and she would never tell something like that. Strange eh?"

Webster nodded slowly, with eyes big as saucers.

"After Medicine Bear gave his stone back, Blue Stone left camp and didn't come back for two weeks. Some folks say he shape-shifted into a wolf and ran from tribe to tribe trying to find all the pieces, but that wasn't it."

The boy was puzzled. He'd never heard the term shape-shifting before and was trying to make sense of it all.

Abe tapped his pipe on the fireplace. "Now then," he said. "This is almost as strange as the eagle being in his teepee. After Blue Stone got back, people he had given the turquoise to started bringing it back to him. They traveled long distances to return them. Some said it caused bad things to happen, others had a dream that told them to give it back, but every piece came back to him--unasked."

That night, after curling up under the covers, Webster dreamt about Blue Stone being a wolf and hunting for those twelve stones. The wolf, the biggest one Webster had ever seen, was nearly all white with ice-blue eyes. It would steal into a teepee and grab the stone in his teeth. Then he would carry it in his mouth while he went on to the next and the next. The scene in his dream changed to a woman stepping out of a ranch house, and the wolf warbling his song for her.

Webster woke from his dog howling for breakfast.

Throughout the years, Webster would see a small band of Indians on a distant ridge moving in quiet parade to and from some encampment. Many times Blue Stone would wave at him across the expanse as he guided his people to the next camp.

He even met with Blue Stone two more times. The boy was eager to hear more stories and, at the first meeting, asked, "How is Hopping Squirrel?" Blue Stone forgave the rudeness of asking the name of someone not present or able to consent sharing it. He replied, "He is called Lame Wolf now. He had a powerful vision and his grandfather gave him his new name."

Webster sensed he had crossed some line and didn't ask any more questions. They talked about their horses and how many people were trampling through Indian lands. They parted with the Indian handshake, grasping each other's arm up to the elbow firmly and looking straight into the other man's eyes.

When he grew older, around nineteen or twenty, he went looking for the camp where he had seen smoke from their fires. At no time did he see evidence of any human beings, or ashes where fires might have been, no areas of flattened grasses or horse droppings.

Even by the stream, the most likely place for a small group to set up camp, not one hoof- or footprint. He decided it was because he was not a good tracker.

Now, a decade after he had fallen from that horse he had relinquished any hope and almost all desire to ever try finding him again, he sat by the stream. He became hypnotized by the constancy of its movement and let his mind go with the water. All thought ceased and only the free flow of being absorbed him.

Across the stream a blurred figure about the size of a large wolf flashed through tall grasses and brought his awareness back.

A wolf didn't step out of those weeds however. A man Webster recognized emerged from the plant life.

"Blue Stone." Lips barely moving, the name wafted out on his breath.

Webster stood nearly as tall as the man across from him and

his blue eyes were beacons shining atop a tanned face framed with a full beard of thick, dark hair, and dark eyebrows. His shoulders were a bit wider than 'average' and he stood as straight as most Indians.

"Boy ... who ... wouldn't ... shoot ... bad ... horse." Blue Stone responded.

The Indian man's face matched his white hair from the burden it carried, but his eyes still gleamed with humor.

"Webster. My name is Webster, and I'm a man now. Have been for some time."

Blue Stone nodded in recognition. "You have been looking for me," the Indian man said. "And now it is *you* that *I* have been looking for. I have a daughter born from the meeting of two spirits. There are white men riding to her house to kill her family, because some Crow braves killed another white family. We will not fight the whites but we will punish the Crow. Many Beads, a woman of my tribe, brought her into the world and was the one to hear the whites gathering outside the trading post and buying kerosene and making torches.

A long silence filled the time they shared, but there was no distance between their hearts. "Our friendship had made it possible for me to ask you—a white—to help me find her and keep her alive."

"Do you know her name?" Webster spoke softly, "Or how old she is?"

"She was born the night the sky fell many seasons ago, Blue Stone answered. "Your people count time in a strange way. I never learned her name, but her mother was called Julia."

Blue Stone answered the questions the best he could then told Webster, "There was fire in their eyes. They will attack tonight or tomorrow. It is a long ride from the trading post to the house they seek to destroy."

"Where is this farm?"

Blue Stone described the area and the best trail to take then added, "There is no man there to protect them."

Those words sparked something in Webster and his heart jumped into action. With urgency, he grasped Blue Stone's forearm with firmness just before he leapt upon his horse, pulled the rein with such force the animal complained, and reared. But before he could dash away, Blue Stone tugged at Web's elbow, and dropped a smooth blue rock that felt strangely warm into his hand.

———————

The riders thundering their way to Savannah's farm were met with a thick fog a few hours before sunset. One man and his horse slammed into a stout oak from the denseness of the fog, convincing them to stop. The chill and damp didn't quiet the fire in their veins, but it would soon be pitch black out even without the fog. They camped for the night with their goal a whole day and part of a nights ride away.

———————

Webster could never have imagined the news that awaited him when he charged his horse straight into the barn.

His brother Jeb strode out with purposeful strides to meet him. A look mixed with sadness and confusion held Jeb's face frozen in a twisted expression.

Webster removed the halter and slowly dropped it to the ground while he tried to read the message on his brother's face.

"What...?" the only word of a longer sentence he could muster.

"Mama ..."

"WHAT!? What do you mean?"

"She was peeling potatoes and just sank to the ground."

"Where's Papa? Does he know?"

"He took a shovel and went to the hill to start the grave. I came back to get the pick axe."

Webster knew he couldn't leave now, or maybe for a few days, even a month would be a better time, but time would not wait for him to save Blue Stone's daughter and her family.

The two men grasped each other in a death-hold for many moments, both shaking with grief, then broke apart, both with blurred eyes, collected the tools needed and rode to the hill to help dig their mother's grave.

The top of the only hill that sat in the horizon surrounding their farm was the spot Flora and Pa had chosen when they first settled here. He had softened the place to four inches down before the boys joined in to try to beat the sun's race to its bed.

It was clear they were losing that race. The grief that they carried made the digging slower. A night's rest would only strengthen their bodies; their spirits could not be healed by sleep.

Starting the next day before dawn and before Pa could manage to rise, the brothers worked quietly and diligently to empty the space before the ground could freeze in the coming days. By late afternoon Pa brought his wife by buckboard up to the hill to be lowered gently into her resting place.

They decided that, between their grief and exhaustion, they needed help to fill in the grave. Jeb rode off to the neighbor that had helped look for Webster so long ago, and he brought two of his sons back. The grave was finished before sunset and they all filed back down the hill to a house that should have been alive with the clanging of pans, or the thumping of bread being kneaded, or chicken being boned. Their lives would be void of the steamy kitchen where their mother boiled their clothes or made preserves. Dishes would pile up in perilous stacks, and the dust and mud on the floor would carpet their house.

Webster could see that disaster coming but couldn't wait to see it happen. Torn between staying to heal the fresh wound still raw in all of their lives, and keeping his word to Blue Stone to try to save his daughter, he paced in the barn unable to decide.

It could be too late already. He thought. *But, a certain amount of decency must be maintained here. I'll ride faster and longer to make up time and wait until the very last minute I can stand.*

Far off in a woody stand, the rising sun warmed the ground, lifting the fog and creating an ever-widening slit of clarity. The men moving about the campsite added to the thinning of the curtain. Each one brought a flour sack and was cutting eyeholes with the light of day. One man had a calico design on his and was ribbed endlessly. They mounted and charged off with the fire still in their bellies.

Webster knew the message had to be given to his brother first. He felt he was betraying his mother, his father and Jeb by standing by his word to Blue Stone. He wrestled with this tangled web most of the day, but managed to tell him by the afternoon.

Jeb looked into his brother's eyes and saw the sincerity and intent. They stood so close that when they lowered their heads, their foreheads touched. They each held their hat the same way, waist high with one hand, the other hand on the brother's shoulder.

"You know all about running this farm." Webster assured his brother and himself, "You know Pa is getting older and won't ask for help when he really needs it. You have to just jump in and take over sometimes. He won't mind, 'cause he likes to see us take charge of things and would brag about it to Ma."

Jeb was tearing up; Webster's voice was cracking. "I don't know if I will ever be back. I made a promise to someone and it's time for me to …"

"Web … please, don't go right now. Wait till Pa's not grieving from losing Ma. It'll be awful hard for him to lose you, too. Please, Web, not now."

Webster grasped his brother's neck firmly and pressed his forehead harder against Jeb's. "Now's the time for you to fill the void that I'll be leaving. You'll be here to help him through his grieving. He can hate me if that's how it will be, but I must keep my promise, like Pa taught us to do."

"What promise? To who? Why's it more important than family?"

"It's best if I just leave it how it is—with you and Pa not knowing all that."

"But, Web, you're talking about abandoning your kin for someone we know nothin' about, at a time when we all need you most. How can you do that?"

"Jeb, I know how it sounds and how it seems, and I really can't explain it, even to myself, but there's a powerful pull on me to fulfill this promise and I know that now's the time to get started."

Stepping back two paces, each reading the other's face Webster's eyes were moist; Jeb's tear was streaking through a light layer of dust and disappeared into his blonde mustache.

Webster spoke through the knot in his throat, "I helped to bury Ma. I got Mrs. Henderson and her daughter to come do the washing and canning. You know everything else to do around here and you do it well. We'll always be brothers, whether I'm standing here or off in some other place we never heard of."

He stayed around until sunset and let the aura of his leaving permeate through to his father's senses. Jeb walked with a stoop he'd never had before and sniffed wet sniffles that he wiped with his sleeve. The brothers didn't speak any more that day. Pa noticed their avoidance and silence. He didn't interfere or ask why.

After the sun vanished the afterglow was enough for Webster to find his way to his father, who was staring toward his wife's grave past the corral. The moon was struggling over the knoll and appeared to pause at the fresh mound. Mr. Michaels recalled how many nights he and Flora had watched the moon rise—too many to count but enough for a lifetime of memories.

"Pa." Webster spoke in his softest voice and stood behind his father.

"Son?"

"Pa …" his voice broke and the words were stuck in his throat, even as the magnet of his destiny pulled its hardest; breaking this bond was taking his breath away.

"You seem to have something you have to do," Pa spoke first. "Your ma was telling me that your heart wasn't on our land anymore. She expected you to leave a long time ago."

Webster was stunned at first—then not surprised. His mother had had a way of seeing into all folks, even those not related. She shocked a neighbor once by congratulating her on being with child before the neighbor herself knew. It must have been the grief that brought these compassionate words and tender tone out of his father.

Pa spoke again, with his usual directness, "Don't s'pose you care to tell me anything 'bout where you're goin', or if and when you might be back. Seems like the last few years you don't have much to say a'tall."

Webster shuffled his feet and dropped his head, "I can't explain it, Pa, I really can't. I wish I could—then maybe I would understand it myself, but it's like being lassoed with a really long rope that's pulling me to … I don't know where." He sounded like the little boy Pa remembered.

"Your ma said it was some kind of fate or destiny had ahold of ya."

"Of course, she'd be able to understand it and speak it better than anyone," Webster said, "but that's exactly how it is—only I don't know what. I don't know if I'm supposed to become a pitchman, or a doctor, or blacksmith or what, but whatever is calling me wants me *now!*"

He was rubbing the stone in his pocket as if hoping the spirit inside would take his pain away. He didn't dare mention Blue Stone and his promise to him. Pa would have taken that as a slap in the face. Besides, Webster really didn't know where his journey would take him or how long it might last.

The marauders met their goal by midnight. Webster was still a full day's ride away.

Eight

Webster at the Dunbar Farmhouse
November 15, 1851

Webster left home with only a vague description of how to find the Dunbar farm. Blue Stone spoke confidently about the landmarks and approximate times to cover the distance, but Webster was unsure. His mind and heart were open to whatever guidance might appear. He uttered the words, "God help me to find this girl alive and deliver her to Blue Stone." The first few hours of his travel, he aimed due south; there were no signs that he was going in the right direction.

He decided to turn to the west at dawn the next day and felt as though a tailwind was urging him onward in that direction. A hawk flew above, leading him by maintaining the same height and distance in front of him and he followed.

Nightfall brought a chill and then a warming from cloud cover. He woke to completely gray skies, the same gray skies that Savannah traveled under. The same sunless, damp feeling filled him. Perhaps her feelings had been so strong she left them trailing behind her.

Breaking camp, he mounted and once again began his journey. When he crossed a wide shallow stream, billows of smoke curled upward beyond the crowns of the trees. He knew it was too dense for a campfire or refuse burning, too dark for field burning, and too confined for a prairie fire; besides, November was not the time of year for prairie fires.

The stench of rotting flesh permeated through his heavy woolen coat and irritated the nostrils of his horse that rebelled at advancing toward the farmhouse. Webster understood and got down.

"S'alright. You stay here. I'll go ahead." The carcass of a horse lay forty paces in front of him

First, he passed the barn, burned down to one third of its size. The heavy doors stood solid as though nothing had happened, but the

44

mow and the stalls were smoldering piles of angry ash, snapping and crackling with vehement tiny explosions.

"I wonder if they started the fire in the house and then ..." talking out loud gave him comfort. He peered inside the barn to assess the contents for any visible human remains and, seeing none, moved on through the yard, past the hen house where a dozen beaks and bodies lay scattered within the framework of what had formerly been their comfortable abode.

The house was still burning in spots, and sending up black smoke of mourning.

Webster approached with complete reverence, even though he couldn't know for certain there were departed souls inside. The chances were great though, and instinct told him there were people within the pyre. Reason had left him, and there was no thought of putting out the fire, but he felt he should stay to care for the remains of whoever was inside when it was safe to do so.

He went back to his horse to find there were now two of them. One had singed mane and tail hair, and obviously singed forelegs, but otherwise seemed unharmed. His horse quickly befriended the wounded stranger.

Webster inspected the new horse carefully and soothed him the best he could before settling in to build a small campfire, which reignited the recent trauma in the horse with its still stinking mane and tail. Webster wrapped a kerchief around the horse's eyes and he slowly calmed down.

The next morning Webster led the two animals to a remaining stack of baled hay for them to feast. The pump still worked and he cleared ash from the trough. Hay and feathers had fallen when the fire created a wind devil, depositing debris and cinders haphazardly around the yard.

Morning fog had quieted the cabin fire that hissed and sizzled in spots but today released white smoke of truce with its feeble demise.

The stone chimney stood defiant, yet obviously impotent to defend the persons within. Some of the family silver or other metal objects had melted, but he saw spoons and other utensils among the debris that gave clues about the life of the people here.

The potbellied stove stood as steadfast as the chimney rock, and except for the charcoal layer on previously shiny metal handles and decorations, it was unscathed. Webster admired the stove and wondered how this humble family could have afforded such a luxury.

The rest of the house lay under the well-constructed roof that now lay nearly perfectly in the shape of gables, but reduced to mere charcoal. He knew what must lie beneath this faux covering.

Why not just leave well enough alone? They need not be disturbed at all. What difference will it make? They certainly won't know...

"*I* will know and they must be cared for," he said aloud.

Moving large sections of the roof proved to be more difficult than the near weightless charcoal boards suggested. He found a crowbar and brought rope, of course, and enlisted the help of both horses to lift the largest workable piece.

There on remnants of a quilt lay a woman whose arms were outstretched toward a smaller form lying face up and looking like a discarded child's doll. But it was life-sized, obviously not a doll.

"Who did this?" He was asking God, like a parent interrogating a guilty child expecting an answer. Lifting each one to remove them to a place of peace, he discovered the woman's hair to be gleaming auburn. Her body had lain over the long braid and the roof had smothered much of the fire so that the floor and anything lying beneath the body was largely intact. Yet, the flesh hadn't been able to withstand the fury of the heat all around it.

Moving the bodies, they each gave up the truth of their demise. The bullets were deep enough within that they hadn't melted in the fire and were now released. When he lifted Julia, a bullet fell onto his boot. He looked down to see what had touched him and a cold chill consumed him. Moments were all it took for him to adapt to the shock, but he prayed that the small body wouldn't reveal such a secret as he gently lifted it into his own arms. A bullet dropped from the child where his heart would have been.

As if in quicksand, Webster slowly sank to his knees and wept. He wept all through the process of placing the bodies into their graves, but by the time the fresh mounds covered them, he was spent. His hopes of saving this family blew away like the smoke and ash on the wind. But he frantically looked for the body of a young woman. He overturned and upended any object large enough to secret her in the house or the barn or the area surrounding the house. She was not found.

Desperation and disbelief spurred him on and he went back in and moved larger pieces of building material. A dresser stood with only the top two layers of drawers burned to ash. The bottom drawers were barely touched by the fire. He opened one of the bottom drawers and found a brown paper used for sending a package. Perfect handwriting addressed the paper to *Savannah Georgia Dunbar – Elk Creek Trading Post.* Up in a corner, smaller in size but written with the same level of perfection, he read: *Aunt Clara – Midlothian, Illinois.*

Maybe she knows where the girl is. He tucked the paper in his shirt, over his heart and next to his skin. Peace washed over him and he felt his search was satisfied.

When he went to the trough where the lone survivor of the fire stood, it ran from him; he determined that the horse wasn't ready to abandon the bonds to this family. Webster left the farm but was so distraught he paid no attention to the direction. The Dunbar's horse ran to the south, and Webster turned north.

All he could think about as he traveled was what form of animosity could possibly be behind such heinous acts. Questions kept rising to the fore: *Why did they not kill the girl? Did she ride away for help and not make it back?*

These questions stayed on his mind, until he came upon Phineas' grave with the dates on it. Now, it was clear why these innocents had no protector and it was probably well known. Anger burned his cheeks.

After two days of riding without sleep, he forced himself to stop. He rolled out his bedroll, pulled off his boots and set his hat on the ground near him and stared up at the stars.

Sleep fell like a 20-pound hammer and by morning the rage was forgotten, but his mission lay ahead. The skies were still gray, giving no clue to the direction he was heading. But he mounted his horse, Alexander, with purpose as though he did know where he was going and stayed the course all that day and half of the next.

It wasn't until then that the sun came out and he could see he was riding in a wide circle. When he came upon some wagons headed westward, he asked what had been their starting point and how were they navigating?

One man stopped long enough to reply, "Comin' outta St. Looey. Heading northwest. Gonna follow the Missourah far as we can. Then, I dunno." Webster noticed he was a wisp of a man, probably from walking most of the way from St. Louis so the wife and two daughters could ride.

"How long you been traveling?" Webster's curiosity was piqued. The answer would give Webster an idea how far he might be from St. Louis.

The stick of a man removed his hat and scratched his head, "Bout three weeks now. River is crooked and Injuns camp near it, so I scoot around 'em sometimes; adds mileage but keeps us alive."

Webster stood up in his saddle, "Do you happen to know which Indians or learn anything about them at all?"

"I come across a bunch at a tradin' post. Owner said they was all Sioux and probably going north to hunt. I don't think I heard any names, though." He turned and looked up at the women in the wagon. "Any of you hear any names of Indians we passed up?"

Silence prevailed for several seconds then the oldest girl spoke up, "Well, I heard someone say something about a medicine man named Medicine Bear. Don't know if he meant that the Indian was around or if he just meant that he knew him somehow."

"Can you remember where the trading post was, I mean how many days back or the name of a town nearby?" Webster asked the man.

"T'was close to ... aw, I dunno where, but it was only a day back—close to the Missourah, like I said."

"Much obliged—good travels to you." Webster was already steering his horse away from the wagons.

He kept his gaze on the ground, looking for unshod horse

tracks or the drag marks of a travois. As he got closer to his goal, more wagon tracks appeared, approaching from many directions. The smoke from the chimney of the post spurred him on.

A stagecoach was sitting outside and the horses were huddled together in the livery. No people could be seen.

Alexander puffed streams of steam while Webster wrapped the reins on the rail.

When he opened the door to the post, a blast of warm air hit him and a burst of laughter met his ears from the half dozen men leaning on the counter or huddled near the stove warming their fingers.

Webster read the faces in the room, searching for the probable owner, but the group assembled was so comfortable in its surroundings that no one man stood out as being 'in charge'.

The blanket covering the doorway of a side room was shoved aside and a man with snow-white hair and bright eyes slipped behind the counter. His beaming smile and clean clothes were clues that Webster had found the owner.

"Howdee doo", he said, "Bud Leaf, and if I don't have it, I'll order it for ya." He stuck out a meaty hand. Webster gripped it firmly and with equal warmth.

"Webster Michaels," Webster replied. "I just heard about your place here and thought I'd take a look around."

"Fine. You're welcome to look, warm up, set a spell. I can make coffee if you like … these boys brought their own firewater. I don't sell it here. Couldn't keep it in stock. Kept getting waylaid by no-accounts. People blame Indians, but it coulda been any outlaw with a thirst."

Time passed with no notice, since there was no sun to change the light. Bud's wife, an Indian woman came out to watch the store and tidy up. By and by, all the other men left and a couple of Indian women came in and traded, with little notice from either Webster or Bud Leaf.

From the expression on Webster's face, Bud could tell there was something on his visitor's mind. During a long pause in conversation, Webster noticed that Bud narrowed his eyes and tipped his head as though listening to some quiet voice.

Webster understood very well. There was a question unspoken. He felt this man was trustworthy and sincere, so quickly decided to tell the older man about his quest. "I started out looking for a young woman about 20 years old, but then I came upon a house where a woman and a young child had been shot and their property burned to the ground. I'm determined to find the murderers." Webster's eyes flashed as he spoke.

Bud said he'd heard something about an Indian raid that left a young girl alive. "Maybe that's her family."

Webster leapt at the information. "I saw a piece of paper with the name Savannah Georgia on it. Was that her name?"

Bud thought for just a second, "No. Her name was Jensen. Went to live with the Gibson's I think."

Those words caused Webster's heart to sink.

"There was another family, lost the father a few years back, a mother and two children. Don't know what happened to them at all. After the father was found dead, none of them came here any more. Don't recall their name, either. Father bought a pot-bellied stove here. Well, traded for it but that was over a decade ago."

"How can you not know his name?" Webster raised his voice. "That must be them."

Bud replied, "I recall his first name bein' told to me. T'was a strange, unusual name. Fontleroy? No. Ferguson ... nah. Oh heck, I can't recall it, too rare a name and too long a time. How's knowin' who they are gonna help you find the murderers anyway?"

"Aw, I dunno. I just get so aggravated about this whole thing. I mean—a baby, barely walking probably—shot in the heart. Why? What kind of a threat could he have been to anyone or anything bigger than a bug?"

They sat in silence for many minutes, the Webster added, "I think you are right, trying to find the murderers is not what I left my home to do. Looks like I'll just head over to Illinois. Well, I thank ya for trying. I'll have to travel a long ways. Is there a place to huddle up tonight? I'll take out in the morning."

"Why, you can bed down right here in front of the fire," Bud offered, "My wife'll bring you whatever you need to be comfortable. We'll share some mutton with you, too."

"I'm going out to see 'bout my horse, then I'll have some pemmican and settle in for the night. Don't want to be a bother. I thank you for everything now, if I don't see you before I go."

The next morning Webster saddled up before dawn and headed for the Mississippi River aiming for Midlothian, Illinois.

Nine

Savannah, Huck, and One Man's Supper

Leaving the river and the raft behind, at the beginning of the ride, she felt like she was struggling against a headwind. Hundreds of wagons were moving the other way, filtering out of crowded townships or failing farms and aiming west. All the wagons were loaded down, challenging the teams' capacities to draw them. Precious family heirlooms vied with staples and necessities for the long passage.

"How will they get across that river?" Savannah empathized with the women and children leaving all comfort on their life-threatening move.

The ride on the raft had been unsettling because she had never stood on anything other than solid ground, except for the time she fell through the ice. Huck and Phineas pulled her out. Nearly falling in themselves. That memory stayed with her for the entire crossing.

Once all the wagons had passed the vista before her was a clear endless expanse to the horizon.

"Huck, I think the worst is behind us. Aunt Clara's is only two days away." The sensation of glorious freedom returned, and she and Huck flew together, blazing their own trail through the high grasses.

They were miles away from the river and all the other travelers, when a stray bullet, probably fired by someone hunting his supper, took Huck out from under her. Savannah never saw the hunter, but she heard the crack of his rifle. The bullet did little damage, as it lodged in Huck's thick haunch, but within a heartbeat, Huck fell, breaking a foreleg so badly the ragged bone thrust through the thin flesh on his leg.

Savannah sat with his head and neck on her lap. When she could no longer bear his groans, she removed the bit and bridle, took his head in her hands, praised him for his steadfastness, and ended his suffering with a single shot in the middle of his forehead. He was the last living connection to life before the devastating night her world ended. Even though she had found the strength to let him go— she wasn't ready and her regret was immediate and deep.

"No!" she screamed, "I'm not ready to be this alone. Stay Old Huck, stay with me." She stayed with him, stroking his mane, keeping buzzards and coyotes at bay, occasionally firing off a shot at one. Wishing she could move back in time and ride off in a different direction or further back and be home with Phineas, Julia, Sean and their farm, she rocked Huck's head in her lap as she searched for the happy times in memories. She suddenly stopped. Stopped wishing, stopped grieving stopped rocking Huck's head.

In this moment, all she knew of her life as Savannah was gone with no hope of returning. She decided that Savannah, as a name, was also gone and determined she would never use it again.

Georgia would be her name now and a new life would begin. She stood up and left the bridle and Huck and walked down the road.

A young girl in a buckboard came along and took Georgia to her own family's farm. The father took two men and they brought the saddle and bridle back to her.

"I don't have any money to pay your for your trouble, but I can stay here and work for you until you feel my debt is satisfied. I'm trying to get up to Midlothian." Georgia spoke softly, thinking of her valiant steed as she held the bridle in her hands and looked at the ground.

"Go ask my wife, Ginny, if she needs any help in the house or with her outside chores. But, for myself, I don't want you to be obliged to me." Those were his words, but his voice was gruff; therefore, what she heard was: "I don't trust no Injun with any bit of my property."

His words held a bit of a sting and to Georgia the meaning was understood. She ignored the slight and did as he suggested by finding his Missus.

"Ma'am, I'd like to be some help to you. I need to buy another … horse …" A lump instantly formed in her throat; she grimaced and swallowed hard and pushed it down, then went on, "… and acquire a few coins to move on with."

The Missus looked up at her. Georgia saw that her eyes held as much sorrow as her own, and maybe more. In addition, they didn't show any sign of abhorrence or rejection for the bedraggled girl in front of her.

"All right," she said quietly, "follow me and I will show you what I need most right now."

Georgia nodded and followed her out to the barn.

"It's planting season and Lucas, my husband, is working in the fields and I have to manage the barn, in addition to the house, the chickens and the garden. We have twin calves and a weak foal to look after." Her voice was crackling from the effects of exhaustion, but she went on. "The foal had a difficult birthing, and the calves will drain their mother, leaving us with no milk at all to use or to sell unless we milk her regular. I need you to keep all the stalls clean; separate the calves from their mother. And milk her and let them feed as you see fit. Watch to see that the foal can stand up and walk around, and keep all the critters fed and the stalls cleaned."

Three sets of dewy brown eyes looked up at Georgia. Their non-judgmental gaze was warm and comforting and a lot like Huck's.

The Missus went back into the house, leaving Georgia with her charges. Days went by. Each night Georgia slept in the barn, curled up in the hay next to the foal, covered with the mare's saddle blanket. She knew the family didn't want her in the house, but at least they were letting her work for money to move on. She preferred being away from people for now and didn't mind not knowing much of anything about this family. The animals were much more hospitable to her and she to them.

She overheard the couple talking one afternoon.

"I can't abide her bein' here any longer," the man said. "Those newborns are getting along fine now and don't need constant attention."

"But *I* need the extra help. I have been able to rest longer in the mornin's because she's doin' mornin' chores." The wife pleaded.

The man growled under his breath, and if Georgia could have seen, he was shaking his head with determination, "But I am *losing* sleep, for two months now, thinking about what she is planning to do to us in the night or what she is gonna steal from me. And I need my sleep and my strength." That seemed to be the final decision and the discussion was closed.

The next day, Georgia said to the Missus, "Moving on isn't going to be as easy as I hoped. I can't earn enough to buy a horse or passage on a stagecoach and I am gleaning that Lucas feels I have overstayed my welcome."

Lucas came up from behind and snapped, "You can be in Midlothian in a week."

"How can I get to there if I don't have a horse?" she snapped back, "Or enough money to buy one?"

"I figger you can hop onto the steamboat, work on it. If you ride it all the way down to New Orleans and back up here or farther, you would make more money—probably enough to buy a horse and whatever else you need." He paused then added. "Guess that would take a mite more than a week."

"What would I do on a boat?" She felt heat rising under her collar and flushing her face.

"I dunno, but they seem to have a lot of folks on 'em. There must be something you can do. Cook, wash dishes. Heck, I dunno."

Just when she was about to disagree, it occurred to her that what he said wasn't such a bad idea. She pondered for a moment. *After all, I don't have to be anywhere. I won't need a horse on the boat. I'm on an adventure, come-what-may, and maybe I could get a glimpse, at least, of those fancy ladies that might live in Savannah.*

She'd earned enough in her barn duties to make coach passage to the next stop. In a nearby town, she bought some food to take on board and got a new hat. Lucas took her to the boat-loading site. When she boarded *The Queen of Natchez* wearing her poncho, her boots and trousers, she quickly slipped by the man with the roster, mumbling, "Name's George Dunbar, I come to work."

She was hired and, in a very short time, made more money than she had ever seen before. However, it also didn't take long until one of the girls from the gambling room discovered 'George' was a woman. Once the man who hired her found out, he put her off the boat. Said he 'just didn't like being made a fool of.'

She had already earned enough to buy a horse, once she got one, she had no idea how near or far she was to Clara's. She only knew she needed to be farther north.

At least the weather will be good. It's late April, she thought as she aimed the horse north and east.

That night the temperature dropped twenty degrees in an hour and went below freezing before midnight.

Too cold and too late to bed down, she thought.

In the deep of the night she fell off the horse and curled up into a ball on the ground.

Ten

Kindred Souls

Wade Clemens had followed a stag miles from the McDaniel's farm. The other farm hands there had driven him to wanting to bump their heads together. He was born free to an escaped slave and had lived and worked on the McDaniel's farm all his life. He was in his forties and most of the farmhands were younger, brash, rude bullies. He kept chasing the deer as an excuse to leave for a time. Besides, all of the hands, including him, were getting tired of chicken and biscuits, no matter how good Missus Ruth could make them.

An hour after the chase began, Wade noticed the deer was not making a good effort at getting away. Rather, it seemed to be leading him somewhere and would stop and wait for him to catch up. That made the game much more interesting. He followed.

Finally, the deer stopped on the far side of a meadow. Wade's fingertips were getting numb from the cold and he wasn't certain he could get a good shot from his position. He dismounted and tread slowly, softly, toward the buck.

"You ready to give it up now? You ain't even winded. I can go all day, but now's as good a time as any to rest."

It stood bravely, unflinching, next to a rock. Wade drew closer. The deer didn't move. Wade could see the buck's breath flow in smoky, visible streams from each nostril. When Wade was twenty yards away, he knew he could get the shot. He raised his gun, but when he cocked it and aimed at the fearless buck, the rock moved. The deer bounded away in long arched leaps into the thick of the woods, while Wade stood in disbelief, the 'rock' moaned and a horse stepped out of the wood line. The hunter turned the rock over and saw a young woman's face. Wade mounted his horse, putting the rock-like woman on in front of him and, leading her horse, returned to the McDaniel's farm.

Mrs. McDaniel's took one look at the near frozen bundle he carried and fired off instructions. "Wade, fill a bucket and get it on the fire. Jesse, go up to the loft and put extra blankets and clean sheets on my bed. Ben and Frank, take care of her horse then come back in and carry her up there." They all moved as ordered. Ruth McDaniel's massaged the bluish limbs and fingers, took off the stiff wet clothes, and stayed by the woman's side throughout the night.

Georgia woke on a day that brought spring back into the climate. Mrs. McDaniels was making breakfast for the farmhands and the smell of coffee, biscuits, and bacon drew Georgia out of the bed.

When she peered down into the lower level, she saw a table made for six with eight men jammed around it. In the middle of the table were platters heaped with the tantalizing bacon and biscuits. An older woman was pouring coffee as she warned, "I don't want one man-boy among you to bother that girl. No flirtin', no teasin' and no rough housin' with her. I hear of any of that goin' on and I'll hand you your hat as I plant my granny's shoe in your backside."

The men kept their heads down, noses nearly in their plates, and to a man said, "Yes, Ma'am."

Once they were outside, Jesse said, "That girl isn't even white. What's the Missus all het up about, anyway?" Frank shook his head and grinned, "Jess, she surmises some of us don't care what breed she is—she is *female*. 'Sides, wait 'til she cleans up a little. You might *be* one of them boys."

Georgia pulled the covers over her head until the men were gone. When the woman came up to see about her, Georgia didn't know whether to thank her for her hospitality or chide her for trying to 'protect' her.

"Well, welcome among the living. What's your name darlin' and where are your people?"

No response. She was willing to answer the first question, but the second was too painful to share with this stranger. Not used to or expecting kindness or trusting to those who appeared to be kind, she kept her gaze to the floor.

"My name is Ruth McDaniels, but you can just call me Ruth, and this is my farm."

"My name? Sav ... Georgia, Georgia Dunbar and I was going to Midlothian, Illinois. Where's my trousers and my horse?" Then she added sheepishly, "Oh, pardon ma'am, um, thank you for taking me in."

"What's your hurry?" Rudeness such as this bristled Ruth and she said with a sarcastic twinge. "Here's your trousers, there's your boots, and your hat's downstairs." Ruth tossed the pants on the bed, took a wide stance and put her hands firmly on her hips.

"Can I pay you," Georgia asked, "or whoever found me and brought me here?"

"Wade found you. He's out in the barn. Go ask him if he wants payment." Ruth decided to let it all unfold without trying to sway things one way or another.

Georgia went out to the barn and found Wade breaking hay bales. When she saw that Wade was a Negro, she wasn't sure what to do or say next.

"Uh, Missus McDaniels tells me you saved me from freezing. I want to pay you for bringing me here and taking care of my horse. But I don't know if ... is that ...?"

"Missy, I didn't save you. It was the Good Lord. He sent one of His masterpieces; a twelve-point buck led me to you. I'm paid well enough here; you don't need to worry. Just find a way to pass it on ... the kindness ... I don't care what you do with the money."

So far, Georgia noted, she had been treated with far more kindness than ever before, and she decided that she had misjudged Missus McDaniels.

After all, this man is comfortable here. She determined that Ruth should be the recipient of 'passing it on' and asked to stay through May to help with spring chores.

Ruth proved to be trustworthy with people's feelings and sincere in her acceptance of Wade and Georgia. After several days of pleasant silence and easy conversation, Georgia asked a question to which she wasn't sure she wanted to hear the answer.

"Ma'am," Georgia began.

"Call me Ruth."

"Yes ma'am. I ... can I call you Missus McDaniels? It ... it just feels better."

Ruth McDaniels recalled her youngest brother and his painfully shy demeanor. No one understood him like she had and as a result he shared his thoughts and feelings with no one else.

"Yes, that will be alright," Ruth replied.

"Well, Missus McDaniels," Georgia continued, noting that 'Missus' meant there was a man somewhere, although she hadn't seen any sign of a Mister McDaniels yet.

"I was wondering about your husband. Is he in the army? I mean, you have a lot of farm here and no man to keep the boys in line."

"My husband works for the railroad. He talks to politicians and landowners to get the rights to put in the rails. He makes a lot of money, so I can pay the boys well, and if they don't act right, they'll lose the best paying job they'll find anywhere. But, yes he is gone a lot, although he sends me money and tools and any new contraption he thinks will make things easier."

"I do see a lot of gadgets here I've never seen before." Georgia smiled as she spun the splines on the eggbeater. These conversations were always brief, but proof that trust was growing.

Later, in April, Ruth's husband sent her a new stove. It took two days, a team of six giant pulling horses, and twelve men to seat it in the house. Then they had to repair the expansions to the doorways needed to get it in there.

Georgia went riding while the clean up and final efforts to nudge the behemoth into position took place. It was the first chance she had had to explore Mrs. McDaniels' property out to its borders. Wade went along as a guide and at the Missus' request.

The air was crisp but alive with the growing spirit of spring as they rode off to the edges of the McDaniels farm. Near the pond a cluster of ducks boisterously complained at the intrusion and splashed into the water.

For the first two hours, she and Wade were silent. For her the smell of springs fresh new growth and the cacophony of birds was conversation enough. Wade knew she needed time and he was willing to give her as much as she needed. He was ahead a few horse lengths. He fell back when the trees and brush got thicker, and then…

"How did you come to the farm, Wade?" Georgia asked.

"My mother bore me on her journey to the north in the Underground Railway. She was afraid we would both be killed if I cried, so she left me with a freed slave at the Morgan Farm south of here. Then she went on her way north."

"What kind of railroad is that? Anything like Mr. McDaniels is making?"

"Well, no. See there are slaves leaving their masters and trying to get to free land. There are people willing to help and shelter them on their way so the slaves won't get caught and probably killed. Those houses and guides are called the Underground Railroad."

Georgia's only reference to these 'kind' people was Missus McDaniel. It was difficult to imagine so many more people like her, when Georgia had not met any.

"Your mother left you with these white people? How …?"

"I know how hard it might be for you to imagine," Wade said, "but all those who are running to freedom are willing to risk their lives by trusting those who are most likely to do them harm."

"Missus is the only white person to show me any respect or convince me she sees me as a human being."

Georgia nodded, Wade continued.

"She has risked a lot too. Not everyone feels like she does, but she has resources to be independent of most other people. I learned from her from the time I could talk. A group of us Negro youngsters were schooled by Missus McDaniels. The others all went off to start their own life. I stayed to work for the Missus for good pay and good food."

"Don't the other men and the neighbors treat you badly?" asked Georgia.

"Missus and Mister McDaniels have always discouraged people from treating me like a slave or worse. Most of the people around are aware of the Underground Railroad and don't interfere with it. A few that go to church with us have shelters for the Railroad on their property."

Georgia was surprised at that and uttered a disbelieving,

"Humph."

Wade went on. "There have been incidents with a few part-time hands, but she sent them packing when they showed any disrespect to me—or to her for standing up for me. Now that I'm a full-grown man, I manage things by myself."

Georgia saw him in a different light, now, too. She believed she now knew someone who could show her how to handle the hatred directed at her by others.

As though he could read her thoughts, he said, "Did you see those ducks back there? When they went into the pond, water splashed all over them from head to tail, but they didn't get wet. They were coated with water, but their bodies didn't hold it. That's how I am with hatred. Folks aim it at me—and I just let it fly past me into the wind."

Georgia smiled and nodded in silent agreement. *Don't know if I will ever be able to do that, but at least I know it may be possible.* Admiration for his courage opened her heart. Its emptiness made her aware of her hunger for human attachment—a long overdue experience she had no idea how to satisfy.

Around noon they sat on soft ground. Sparing their 'sit' bones further abuse by the saddle, they drank water and gnawed on some jerky. She dusted a tick off her boot and looked up at Ward. The words popped out with no restraint.

"My mother and younger brother—he was only four—were killed before my eyes and our farm burned by 'church' people because *my* father is Indian." She watched Wade's expression change. At first he was stunned, then empathy softened his face and his heart.

She went on, "I haven't found many folks that didn't get that look of fear or disgust as soon as they laid eyes on me. In addition, nobody ever told me how to *be* or what to do when that happens. Phineas, the man who raised me, never stopped me from showing how I really felt about them, and he taught me to use that energy for chopping wood or digging post holes."

She noticed Wade tilt his head, leaning what must have been his good ear toward her. She continued. "I admire your ability to ignore the indignities heaped upon you, but I don't think it's natural...I guess I mean it wouldn't be natural to me."

"How so?" he said.

"You know back there a ways I saw a trap with a fox foot in it. No fox, just the foot. You and I know how that happened. He wasn't going to stay there in pain and starve to death. He let his foot go to save his miserable life. That's how I deal with it." Georgia felt a wave of rage rising inside her belly, but her heart was full of compassion for the animal, and her head was fighting a losing battle to keep it all down.

"But don't you have people that can help you out of your trap?" Wade replied.

"Never there when I've needed them most," she snapped and immediately regretted those words. "Besides, I don't believe they are *my* people. I don't have any people that would help me. You were put in a place that took you in, like Moses. I came out of my mother in a place that hated everyone that looked like me."

"My people are hated, too. Surely, you know that. "

She did know that. Their similarity was the reason she felt she could talk to him.

Wade was still talking. "It's just a part of our life. Sure, I feel the sting and even taste the venom they spew, but I don't hold on to it. It does no one any good to ..." He stopped, realizing that the difference in their experiences couldn't really be compared.

His voice softened and he went on. "You're what, nineteen? Life will only get more difficult for you if you can't let it all go and find a 'people' that you can feel at home with." He watched closely for a reaction. "Maybe it's the Indian side of you that needs to find a place of belonging. And I'll bet that right now you're thinking that's the last thing you want. But ask yourself if maybe that isn't just exactly what you need?"

"Oh, you are so right about my feelings toward my 'Indian side'. That's the cause of all the misery in my life, and yes, the only reason I'd ever take up with them is to find my real father and find ways to make him as miserable as I have been."

"Georgia, God willing, you have a lot of time to deal with that hatred part of yourself. I hope you don't harm others while you're wrestling with your own soul. In the meantime, trust me to help you in any way I can."

"I know, Wade. I've never said any of these words to anyone else, not even my mother. She tried to tell me she 'loved' the Indian that was my real father. I can't believe that. It just didn't make sense to me. How could she? No one else in the white man's world seems to love Indians. The monsters that killed her and my brother did so— without blinking—just because *I* lived among them."

Wade mounted up and she followed his lead. Moving forward changed the mood. Mention of her mother brought memories of her and what the two of them would be doing now. An image of empty cellar shelves came to mind. Mother would be chatting about what to plant in the house garden so the shelves would be refilled in the fall. She recalled their garden and how the rabbits would ravage it and she grinned as she thought about the cat they'd had. It had seemed to like the rabbits and wouldn't chase them off.

She kept smiling with thoughts of sitting in the garden, shooing away rabbits, writing in her diary and breathing in deeply the smell of rich Iowa earth. *Mother would be hanging out the wash, mimicking chicken talk as she fed the hens, and she'd be singing.* The memory was so strong she could hear Julia singing. Her memory replayed that vision for the rest of the day.

Eleven

Listen to the Small Voice

"I'm taking you to church with me this Sunday." Missus McDaniels announced when Wade and Georgia returned. Georgia's countenance turned a few shades lighter and her astonishment surprised the Missus. She bubbled out a laugh and said, "Well, good heavens, girl, I didn't ask for a limb! I just wanted to let you know that I intended to take you to church."

Georgia hadn't told Ruth anything about her situation or that 'church people' had caused her to be without a mother and her little brother. She liked Ruth—a lot—even admired her, but Ruth's determination to take her to church put Georgia on the defensive.

"I'd rather not go to church if you don't mind, Missus." Georgia was speaking softly but wanting to shout.

"Well, the minister won't baptize you before you leave, if that's what you're concerned about. I just thought it would be nice for you to meet some young people your age and spend some time with them for a while."

It was clear that Ruth wasn't going to take no for an answer and she added, "I have a nice dress that I can fix to make it fit you. It won't take long. You might want to shine up those boots. Even though Sunday is a few days away, those boots need a lot of work and I'm giving you lots of notice."

Georgia shined up her boots Saturday night and when she put them on Sunday morning, she slipped a knife in her boot next to her right ankle. The spirit infused into her genes insisted she take the knife. The inner voice was strong to the point of being nearly audible. What else could she do?

At the church Wade sang in the choir and Missus played the piano, while most of the farmhands crowded in the back row looking like children waiting for punishment. Georgia sat as close to the door as possible, across the aisle from unruly boys with uncombed hair. A few pews up she noticed a hat with a large fluffy raccoon tail hanging down the side.

After the service Georgia found that people were a lot friendlier here and the minister seemed to be truly humble. She felt welcomed when he looked her in the eye as he greeted her with no hint of deception. However, she still pulled her hand away quickly when he enclosed it with both of his.

A woman who reminded her of Julia invited her to visit in the afternoon.

"Thank you ma'am, but I like to just ride in the afternoon. Give the horse exercise and clear my mind a while. But, thank you for the invite." Georgia was sincerely thankful. If she weren't, she would have said nothing.

The young people Missus spoke about weren't so accepting. They didn't stare like she was accustomed to, but they didn't make any moves in her direction, either. One man, about twenty, had noticed and overheard Georgia's plans for the afternoon. However, he concealed his interest and was the first to ride off. He watered his horse in the stream near the church until Missus McDaniels and her company left for home. He knew where her farm was and was willing to wait for Georgia to be riding alone, unguarded, to make his moves.

In the afternoon Georgia rode out as planned to some of the places Wade had pointed out were good for communing. She could feel that the ground was soggy from just thawing, which made riding slower than she liked. However, it gave her a chance to inhale the smells of all the new blossoms and hear the beehive and the woodpeckers work echoing in all directions. Another sound—not of nature—followed her. There was no mistaking the pattern of hoof beats and the same 'something' that told her to bring a knife, told her to pretend not to notice, but she couldn't deny it for long.

Georgia saw the young man from the church coming towards her while he was still some distance away. Although she supposed most considered him a man, he had the stature of a boy. He was still in his neat and mostly clean Sunday clothes and the hat with a raccoon tail attached. She had noticed his hat at the church and she thought he probably hadn't taken that hat off since the day he put it on. It seemed the stains were holding it together. The tail waved in the wind as he rode to intercept Georgia.

He made other mistakes that any white man who didn't hunt for a living would make. To Georgia's ears, he might as well have been shouting his presence. She stayed as much in the open as the woods would allow, but kept on riding. When he startled a flock of small birds, she turned around.

"Come out or ride on away from me. You're disturbing my peace," she demanded. He came out from the woods with his pistol pointed at her. The expanse between them provided her a full view of the woods, half of the field in front of her, and a hawk circling above. She noticed it; he didn't. Her mind was working on a strategy that would keep her unharmed under the circumstances. Nothing came to mind except, *Knife. Gun. Knife. Gun. Knife.*

The gun owner had a mouthful of very bad teeth. He grinned at her as he eyed her up and down. Georgia never thought to ride away. Circumstances seemed to have conspired to bring this about. Besides, a one-on-one confrontation with a white man her own age felt like the fulfillment of a deep wish.

She kept the horse still as the man galloped across the gap between them, his pistol still in hand and the raccoon tail flapping rapidly as he rode toward her.

"If you want this horse," she said, "you can't have it. It ain't mine. You'd be stealing from the McDaniels and they would put you in jail. I have no money or other valuables with me. What do you want?"

He just laughed and kept riding.

"That's what I was hoping you'd say," she said and dismounted, putting her horse between his aim and her, betting he would value the horse's life over hers and not shoot it.

She kept maneuvering the horse between them as he zigged and zagged, trying to get her back in his sights. He gave up on that tactic and got off his horse angry and frustrated. His face was red and screwed into a vicious scowl when he landed three feet away. Georgia took advantage of his lack of concentration, pulled the knife out of her boot, and swung her foot high to kick the gun out of his hand. He grabbed the heel of her boot when her leg was extended; she fell to the ground backward. Her knife hand was pinned behind her back. He undid his pants and wrestled with her skirts. The raccoon tail hung over his shoulder and covered both of their cheeks.

Looking up past the brim of his hat, Georgia saw a shadow coming out of the sky. The man-boy let out a horrible shriek. Blood poured down his face and onto hers before he was able to stand. He was screaming and flailing at the hawk with one hand and clutching his face with the other. His blood painted the white streak in her hair with red and ran down her cheekbone toward her ear. When she stood, it ran to her chin.

The hawk grabbed that raccoon tail, the hat and a piece of flesh and flew off. Its talons had scraped a double furrow on the man-boy's face in the process. While he had both hands to his face, Georgia stood, picked up his pistol, emptied the contents in front of him, and then threw the weapon back toward the woods. The hawk had lost a few tail feathers in the fracas, the kind that couldn't be replaced soon. Georgia picked them up.

"You know why that hawk took after you? He wanted your hat. Guess you won't be wearing such decorations on your head from now on." She waved the knife menacingly and continued, "I really wish it was me that took that piece of your scalp. Maybe I'll get a piece now."

The man-boy squirmed and let out a squeak. In truth, all she wanted was to hear him squeak. He scrambled to his feet and ran towards his horse in the woods. She watched as he rode away.

At first she was simply grateful to the hawk for saving her, and then she began to relish the satisfaction of retribution for many wrongs done to her, and to Julia and Sean. Once those feelings arose, she discovered it was a bottomless pit which could never be filled. It just wasn't enough and she wanted to cause more pain. As she envisioned torturing, maiming, slashing and bashing others, she saw her hatred take on a life of its own, and even with all of her concentration, she could not make it stop. And when it did stop, it was because her mind replayed the acts done by the killers of her family. Next to that she saw herself carrying out those things she had just imagined doing to them. There was no difference and she could see that.

She realized there would be no satisfaction in retribution. Like a spoiled child, she wanted that and became furious from the denial of it. Tears that burned with the fire of her fury and disappointment stung as they seared a path down her face. They mixed with the blood of her attacker and the two merged into a grotesque painting on the dark brown canvas of her skin. The strange smearing of watercolor tattoos on her face and neck marked her as though she was one of those 'monsters' dictated to by their hatred.

She mounted her horse with a triumphant flourish and rode back to the farm.

Frank saw her first from a distance, and then closer, with blood all over her hair and face. His eyes popped wide. "Wade, get the Missus," he shouted.

At first glance everyone assumed the blood was hers and a flurry of action got the men moving in all directions: to pump water, find clean rags, and do a two-man carry to get her to the house. Georgia was gloating inside from her victory and luxuriating in all this fuss. She decided not to tell them she wasn't hurt, and she wasn't sure what all the fuss was about.

Missus came running but not out of panic. She met the men carrying Georgia and calmly directed them to put her on the rug near the fire. Once the men settled the 'patient,' Ruth inspected the apparently wounded area and saw no open gash.

"You'll be just fine once we clean you up," she said.

The men had provided three full buckets of water, far more than was needed. Missus thanked them graciously and eased them out of the door.

"That's real fine, boys. You go on now. We thank ya." She turned to Georgia. "Tell me now, if you can, what happened?"

"This crazy no-account from the church… had a raccoon tail on his hat. And while he was on top of me …" Georgia began to laugh, Ruth wasn't sure if it was laughing or crying because she knew sometimes both happen at once. Ruth waited patiently for the mix of emotions to be sorted out and for Georgia to let it go.

Georgia was thinking how providence had fooled them all and played with them like puppets. The hawk was fooled by a disembodied tail of a raccoon; the man-boy was fooled by thinking she was a lot less than she really was, and she fooled herself by thinking she could take care of herself at all times.

"We are all just a bunch of dolts," she said as she laughed.

Ruth was not smiling or laughing when she asked, "Did he enter you?"

Georgia had to think about it, and her laughter stopped abruptly. "Everything happened so fast and he was pulling my clothes …" she answered. It was then that the timing of the hawk seemed directed by an unseen master. Not unlike the deer that had guided Wade to her near-frozen body or the appearance of Huck when she'd needed him most.

She looked into Ruth's eyes and saw the sincerity and nurturing intent within them. It reached the place that so needed it— Georgia's heart. Tendrils of human bonding began to tickle their way in with silken threads. She was compelled to cut them off. What made it all right to allow those to grow with Wade and not with Ruth was a question that would be unanswered for a long time.

"No," she said calmly, completely composed now, and turned away from Ruth. "He didn't … a hawk attacked him. The blood all belongs to the no-account."

During the next week, Georgia withdrew from everyone. She didn't ride in the afternoons or evenings, and she didn't speak more than three words at a time to anyone. Ruth asked Wade to try to reach her. He reported back with no success.

Her silence was not intended to shut everyone out. It had the benefit of giving her time to look inside again as the mirror of her mind had shown her. By day she kept reminding herself that vengeance and retribution made her like those she despised. At night she dreamed a series of dreams, trying to work it all out. With each dream she became better at holding her anger.

Finally, one night she had one of *those* dreams, one that was so real it was hard to convince herself it was only a dream. It began in that field just before the man-boy got within arm's length. He was aiming for her with his body and his gun. She looked to the sky and called to the hawk. It came down and landed on her arm. The villain was so shocked that he got on his horse and rode off without ever touching her.

She woke, dressed quickly, and rode out to find the hawk. She rode past the pond where dozens of yellow ducklings had sprouted, rode on over plowed ground, inhaling earthy perfumes, and on past the farthest edge of tamed earth. From the time she took the reins in her hand, she carried a sense that every move she made was perfectly in tune with something meant to be; fate was in control and she let the horse do whatever it wished.

He ran quickly for a while then slowed until he brought her near to—if not actually to *the* place—where she was attacked.

The horse began walking slowly, finally coming to a complete stop. Its rider kept her gaze to the ground. She had the hawk's feathers in her hat now. When she looked up, the scene was exactly like her dream. The angle and intensity of the light, the shape of the tree line, the smells—everything was the same. And the hawk was circling above.

Just as in her dream, she raised her arm and called out, making a sound as close to his as she could. "Screeee, screeee" The bird began to descend. She called again. Reality and dream were merging. The beautiful freedom she felt in the dream was being born in this waking moment.

What is that drumbeat in my ears? It's in my chest. "Is he … could he …? Yes. Please, come closer."

The hawk screed again and spiraled downward. It was making smooth, wide circles in syncopation with the pulse of the communing of earth and sky. She held her breath, wishing it closer, in awe of its powerful grace. It was two feet above her when it raised both wings to their full height and stretched its legs with steely talons curled toward her. She was breathless. Quickly she wrapped the leather reins around her arm to protect her from his well-honed talons. He landed on her wrist. Joy streamed down her cheeks; her heart was bursting with it. Time did not exist now.

The bonds she denied to fellow humans rushed forth to seal the mysterious connection with her totem. She stroked its back, admiring every gleaming feather. Then she inspected his tail; it was confirmed—he was missing a few large feathers, the kind that can't be replaced. This was the same hawk, her hawk.

He blinked his inner lid, then the outer layer and then stood regally straight up. The talons were pressing into her flesh through the leather straps, but she was willing to endure the pain to the end of this experience.

She looked at its beak and laughed. "I mean you no disrespect, but your beak looks just like my uncle Harley's. Should I name you that? Harley? It will give honor to the name at least."

The hawk raised its wings and brought them back down quickly. She interpreted that to be a shrug.

"I don't know why you are befriending me, but I accept. As long as you choose to be my friend, I will be yours."

She dug into a saddlebag and offered up a piece of chicken. The gift was accepted. The bird took it and flew to a low branch within her sight to tear at it. The quickness with which her gift was devoured told her it was much relished. The bird looked at her while he enjoyed each morsel. It was an expression of gratitude, and she felt it.

She mounted the horse, and as she rode away, a voice in her head—the voice of a man—clearly said to her, "The hawk has shown you how to rise above those who would harm you in spirit. You, too, must practice rising above."

Twelve

Time To Go

She stayed on the farm for a few more weeks. The sense of freedom the hawk had reawakened in her would not be still. Neither would the feeling of being completely in the hands of fate, doing its bidding. On a ride to visit Harley one morning, she noticed spring had quickly moved toward summer. All the ducklings were brown and indistinguishable from their parents. All the trees wore green. The ground was no longer mushy. Accents of purple lupine and unnamed yellow blossoms proclaimed spring to be at its height. Most of the spring farm work was finished and soon it would be time for the summer farm hands to show up. Her spirit felt a nagging tug day and night.

All evidence pointed to the hands on the invisible clock within. *It's time to go.*

"Missus McDaniels, I'm going to head out down the river again. I hope to make some money on the boat, then come back up and get to Midlothian to Aunt Clara's. I'm not sure what I'm going to Clara's for or what I will do on the boat, but something is urging me to go." Georgia stood beside Ruth, watching her strong, ragged fingers dress a chicken.

"I've seen it coming. Don't think I won't worry about you 'cause I will—every day. You can write, you know? I ain't goin' anywhere. Maybe you can come back next spring and help out. You're a good worker and I promise I won't ask you to go to church again!" They laughed. Ruth's eyes twinkled noticeably when she laughed.

"I like to hear Wade sing," Georgia said, "so I might just go anyway."

Ruth went on. "You tell Wade you're goin'. It wouldn't be fair for me to surprise him with it when you're gone." She wiped her hands on the floor-length apron and tucked up a wisp of her hair. Her hands were clean and her arms were free to embrace the girl standing next to her. But she waited for the girl to take one more step toward her.

Georgia did not take that step.

"Yes, I'll tell Wade, Georgia said. "I have some things I want to tell him. A long silence stretched between them and Georgia felt bonding tendrils reaching toward her again. She shuffled her feet and quickly turned away from Ruth. She took several steps toward the door then stopped short, and without turning around, she said, "Missus, I don't have the words to thank you proper. I do believe you know what words I want and ought to say to you ... I owe you my life. And it just may be that I can come back here next spring to help with all the work."

"See that you do." Ruth took the opportunity to end the tension and went back to denuding the chickens. Georgia hurried out the door to find Wade without looking back.Wade was in the barn repairing a bridle when Georgia came in. The smell of linseed oil had overtaken the hay and manure odors that usually overwhelmed her. It was a pleasant change.

"Wade ... I ...," she choked.
He spoke for her.

"You're leaving and come to say good bye and maybe thank me," he said. "But you don't know how to say all that and you don't want me to try to talk you out of goin'."

"Ain't no way you could talk me out of it. And I have more than that to say. The hawk, the one that saved me from... It's out beyond the south pasture, hangs out in that stand of birch trees. I named him Harley and he likes Missus' fresh fried chicken or even the innards. Just to keep him kinda friendly, could you visit him sometimes and talk to him? He saved my life."

Wade stared at her as though trying to see into her mind and make sense of what she had just said.

Georgia continued. "I don't know if he'll come to you, but he sets on my arm and I talk to him. He don't seem to mind ... so just take him some good food once in a while and maybe he'll save your life someday, too."

He nodded.

"Well, I've got to get to the river so I can get hired on to one of those fancy boats. I may be back next spring. I really don't know. Another thing about the hawk, you'll know it's him by the missing tail feathers. They haven't grown back—never will. But he seems fine without 'em. Guess we're all missing a few feathers or carrying scars of one kind or another."

Wade nodded again and watched Georgia ride away.

Thirteen

Georgia on the Mississippi

The Mississippi was nearly clogged with all the boats, and to her ears, the paddle wheel on her boat sounded like a waterfall. Boatmen called out the depths of the river over the swooshing wheel that propelled the ship smoothly along. Fish smells mingled with the heavy odor of silt; she loved such strong, earthy aromas. Whenever she could steal a few minutes from her work, she hugged the rail and watched deer, elk, and wolf drink at the edges and dash off to safety.

This boat was equipped with a 'Ladies Cabin'. Her job this time around required her to wear a dress, an apron, and a starched little cap. No more boots—but bloomers were required. The Ladies Cabin was meant to keep the women occupied in palatial surroundings while the men caroused and gambled. Ornate carvings, marble table tops, gold decorations and statues assaulted Georgia's senses such that she could barely look at them very long.

Scrubbing the floors, dusting the ornate décor, and serving the ladies showed her how tied to the earth she really was. None of this work felt useful or part of 'being' a child of the earth. The pay was beyond her wildest dreams, but stories of other boats exploding, burning, and sinking for no known reason kept her from getting good sleep.

When the boat pulled to shore to load and unload some passengers at night, Georgia got off to regain her land legs and looked back at the boat.

The last stop before Memphis, a saloon girl in a sparkly dress walked up beside her and started talking to her like they were old friends. "There is nothing prettier than this river boat all lit up at night and glittering up the water. Her lights shine and the water ripples out twelve times more of them. Did you notice the chandelier in the gambling room?" Neither of them were looking at each other.

76

Georgia let her go on.

"It has crystal droplets that make delicate music when the boat rocks just right. Makes me think that angels or good spirits of some kind are around. 'Course, angels wouldn't be caught within a hundred miles of that sinful place."

Georgia smiled at the woman's perfect description of the boat. The woman smiled back and gave her a friendly look, before returning to listen to the chandelier. Alone again. Georgia turned her back to the river and scanned the tree line. A scythe of a moon was sitting in the tops of the trees, and a star an inch away seemed to be thinking of slipping into the moon's cradle. *How many nights did Mother stand at the corral waiting for the moon while the coyotes or wolves sung the moon up into the sky? I always believed they were greeting each other ... and the night."*

Moments of such reverie were few on the river. She wrote in her journal: *The passengers don't mix well with each other, especially after consuming whatever sorts of spirits are available. The backwoodsmen bring their own moonshine aboard, and the high stakes gamblers drink the expensive assortment in the saloon. Both groups take strong offense to each other—and me, of course.*

Georgia discovered that she was not the only target for displeasure. In fact, it was the Negroes working on the boat who earned the most scorn from everyone else. They weren't like Wade. He was comfortable in his skin. The Negro men on this boat carried themselves differently and seemed to try to disappear into the background. Except for Franklin.

He was the biggest man Georgia had ever seen anywhere. He lifted cotton bales and wooden crates single-handedly; all the other men needed help. He also had a temper but, because of his size, was rarely challenged or called out for it. Franklin had a child of about twelve named Ebony Rose, who was already sewing and learning to cook. Georgia cleaned the ladies cabins and kept fresh sheets on the beds; Ebony taught her how to sew.

Well, she tried.

Georgia wasn't used to such detailed work and didn't take to it. Every time she poked herself with the needle she'd throw the whole project across the room. Ebony just shook her head and picked it up and started over. The first time it happened, Ebony said, "Didn't your momma teach you not to get so angry?"

"No. And my father didn't, either. They just let me be. I couldn't stop myself and neither could they." Georgia would try again the next day, poke herself, and throw the skirt or blouse across the room again. After a week with no improvement, Ebony didn't offer to teach her to sew any more.

The farther south they traveled, the atmosphere on the boat became increasingly tense.

Passengers who boarded were more belligerent to the Negroes. Franklin and his fellow workers didn't like it. They complained to each other in private, but they all knew there was nothing they could do about it. Georgia knew what unexpressed anger did to a body, but she, too, knew she couldn't protest such treatment. What made it worse, the captain seemed to sense Franklin's resentment and responded with more terse commands.

"Boy! Get that man's bag! Boy! Load them crates like I told you and be quick about it, then shine my boots 'til I can see my face in 'em." Even though Franklin was the captain's favorite, he knew Franklin wouldn't buck his commands in front of the white men or he'd be fired, or worse.

Franklin took the results of that attitude ashore. Georgia watched him storm off the boat, swinging his fists and punching the air, fighting an invisible demon. For her eyes only, a noticeable darkness dropped like a curtain in the bright light of day as she watched him disappear into the crowd. She could feel it had deep meaning but didn't know how to interpret it.

That night a ruckus at the back of the boat woke her. She wrapped up in a blanket and went out. The paddle wheel was shushing, but everyone kept talking at once above the peaceful influence of the water.

Mabel, the saloon girl, was shouting at the captain, "You can't just let him float away. He has a little girl here, with no mama, and she deserves to be able to say goodbye to her father. You have to stop and go get Franklin."

Georgia's jaw dropped when she deciphered, "can't let him float away,' 'say goodbye to her father,' and 'stop and go get Franklin.'

The captain sneered at Mabel, smacked her on the behind, and said, "Why, Mabel, I don't think I've ever seen you so riled. Makes me want to …"

Mabel punched him hard in the chest and turned away, crying.

"Franklin attacked a white man," the captain added. "You know we saved him from a lynching."

When she passed near, Georgia grabbed her arm. Mabel took a one-eighty swing at her before she realized who it was. Her eyes were filled with tears, Georgia ducked, Mable missed.

"Sorry, Georgia I didn't realize it was you."

"What happened?" Georgia whispered with intense interest.

"Ebony's father was wrapping ropes," Mabel said. "Near by, some of the male passengers were standing at the rail talking. One man, fat, wearing a fancy suit, round, big moustache, says to a tall woodsman in buckskins—Franklin was near, within earshot—fat man says, 'You hear about the white man got hung for killing a slave?' "The man in buckskins noticed Franklin—and Franklin's annoyance at the fat man's rudeness. He answers, 'No, can't say as I did.'

"The man in the suit says, 'Since I am a gambling man, I bet the sound of that statement is music to your ears. I also bet you're one of those abolitionist blowhards trying to ruin this country.'

"The man in the buckskins says, 'What if I am? And whether or not I'm abolitionist, it sounds t' me like some kinda justice were done.'

"The man in the suit shoots a sideways glance at Franklin. 'May be. You see, the fellow they hung had destroyed another man's property. Killed one of his slaves … so they hung him. That's *my* idea of justice for sure!' Mabel's voice was shaking with emotion.

"I guess after years of being a slave, then carrying bags, shoveling coal, hauling heavy rope lines, moving freight and getting only insults Franklin had had enough. With his huge, dark hand he grabbed the man in the suit by the throat and lifted him off the ground. But before he could come back to himself and set the man down of his own accord … two other passengers pulled him off, then grabbed Franklin and threw him overboard." Mabel began crying as though her own father had been tossed over. The empathy and deep well of grief in Georgia was beginning to erupt; but she held it by saying, "You go on. I'll tell Ebony in a while."

Georgia knew what years of unspoken resentment could do and defended Franklin in her thoughts as she tried to keep her composure. *I'm glad I didn't cut or stab the no-account that jumped me in the field, but the time may come …*

She stopped herself as she remembered what a bottomless pit that was and tried to prepare herself to tell Ebony about the tragedy. The overwhelming pressure to cry kept forcing its way through her body.

How do you tell a twelve-year-old, motherless Negro child that lives on a boat that her father, her only known living relative, is dead and no one would retrieve the body?

Ebony was awake and getting dressed when Georgia entered the small cabin. Maybe the noise had disturbed her sleep, maybe the heated and dark atmosphere on the boat the last few days forewarned her. Ebony looked at Georgia—deep into her soul and beyond—with eyes that seemed to go on forever. Sadness was only one of a rich collection of feelings and qualities Georgia found in Ebony's eyes. Wisdom, kindness, patience, love resided in that soul.

When the sadness Georgia was trying to hide met the compassion and sadness in Ebony's eyes, their hearts united.

The tenderness Georgia intended to give to another was instead given to her. Just a gentle nudge of the door on Georgia's heart, rusted shut from holding back a mountain of unshed tears—a nudge by one who truly understood that the source of the pain was a result of pure hatred—released those tears. She crumbled to the floor, Ebony reached for her and Georgia was sobbing in Ebony's arms. Ebony matched the sobs breath for breath and their tears mixed on each other's cheeks.

They clung to each other until their sorrow was spent and Ebony rocked Georgia while she wept soft tears and prayed silently with all her heart for them both.

Over the next several days, Georgia and Ebony shared many hurts they'd had in their life. Ebony's mother had died a year before she and Franklin started living and working on the boat.

"Mama was always very thin, and I was the only child she birthed alive. We don't know what she was sick from, but Papa knew she was dying and told me to be sure that I didn't do or say anything that I would feel sorry for when she went to heaven."

As she listened to Ebony's life story, Georgia better understood the connection that sealed them. She cringed inside a little at the mention of 'heaven,' but left it alone. Some of the saloon girls sent the Negro cook, to Ebony's cabin to offer condolences. The cook mentioned each one who had offered. They couldn't know that Georgia was vicariously sharing in the tender feelings.

Two days later the boat drifted into a port in the afternoon; the light was soft, the trees were wearing lacy shawls of living filigree that swayed in unison with the slightest breeze. Georgia was enchanted. Back home, her favorite tree was a willow, stroking the water with its graceful arches and fingerlets, moving like that ... *They must be related,* she thought.

The boats stacks announced in bombastic form that the destination had been reached. A shipmate walked past and she shouted over the blast to him. "Where are we?"

"Natchez. Where did you want to be?" he shouted back.

"Savannah."

"You got on the wrong boat, on the wrong river, in the wrong state. Good luck." And he hefted his sack over his shoulder as he walked away into the bustling port of call.

I never asked where this boat was going. I thought they all went to Savannah, she realized.

Her plan had been to go to Savannah, then on to New Orleans and back up to Illinois and Aunt Clara's. She figured that would give her enough money to continue.

That had been two weeks ago, when Franklin was still alive. Now the plan was to get up to Clara's as soon as possible, taking Ebony there and finding a home for her. Harley would never stand for having a Negro child in his house, but Clara was friendly and well-known in the town. There were freed families there, too; Clara had told her she was teaching them reading and writing in the church basement at night.

There was only one thing left to do—tell Ebony the plan. A saloon girl had braided Ebony's hair and was giving her a hug when Georgia walked into the room. Georgia smiled at her as she headed for the door.

"Thank ya, Ebony darlin', for fixin' my dress," the girl said and quietly closed the door.

Before Georgia could speak, Ebony said, "I had a dream about my father last night. He told me I should go with you. Are we leaving now?"

Georgia looked at the child before her, wise far beyond twelve years, and marveled at the ability to accept whatever life threw at her. Listening to dreams and voices that whispered to the heart was something else they had in common. This child, still unschooled in formal learning, knew the secret to surviving in a world that worked against her.

"How can you do that?" Georgia asked. "Just leave here, trust in me to take care of you ... and ..."

"But it isn't you that's taking care of me. God puts all that happens to me and all the people that come into my life there. My mama taught me that and proved it to me many times. I was sad and scared when my father was killed and I let all the sadness out to make room for whatever good things were coming. You were there. Right then, God sent you."

Georgia wouldn't argue by sharing her own examples of how she thought God treated people. If it had any effect on Ebony, it would have been to dishearten her, and that was the last thing this beautiful child needed. Besides, the grief they shared together had been healing for Georgia, too, and could not be denied.

"Yes, we'll be leaving as soon as I can wangle a horse and saddle with the money the captain owes me. He owes you some for sewing, too, don't he?"

"I usually just trade. The men give me—well—they gave things to Franklin. He didn't want any of the men anywhere near me if he wasn't around. They gave him whatever they could find that I might need, and the women do my hair, bring me ribbons, buttons, pretty things." Ebony smiled a warm smile and patted her fresh braids.

"All right, I'll get my money and buy a horse. Oh, we're going to Illinois to see my Aunt Clara. She'll find a family for you, if that's what you'd like."

They left at the next boarding stop. The weather was good. They had a good horse and Georgia had lots of food in the saddlebags. Everything worked out well in getting ready; a sense of relief filled both of them as they left the past behind them. As the day wore on they realized that neither of them knew anything about the lands they were in. Ebony had come up from Louisiana, from bayous, swamps and thick growth. Georgia was from the plains, where she knew how to find prey and make shelter. Now they were in an area fed by the river, a river that frequently flooded, washing away promising seedlings and leaving behind thick murky silt.

Georgia got off the horse several times to lead it and keep it from sinking too deep into the mire. Near night and still no decent shelter in sight, Georgia decided to sell the horse, keep the saddle, and buy passage on a northbound boat. However, for this night, they would have to snuggle up under the biggest tree they could find.

Ebony collected some firewood while Georgia prepared a spot to lie in and attempted to dry it out by tossing dry soil on the damp dirt to absorb the cold, wet, earthen mattress they had to sleep on.

Instinctively, they were both quiet as they moved about in this strange land. Whenever a twig or larger branch snapped, Georgia pulled her gun and motioned to Ebony to hide the best she could. It was usually a raccoon; once it was a deer's antlers snapping off dry sprigs over its head.

Not long after they were settled and ready to sleep, they heard several twigs snap and leaves being crushed. Only one creature could be making those sounds. Georgia reached beside her and uncovered her pistol from the layer of leaves she had used to hide it.

"Keep as still as if you were dead," she whispered directly into Ebony's ear and put the blanket over her small form as if it were merely a blanket, piled haphazardly.

The sounds of movement kept approaching. Georgia found herself becoming increasingly calmer as the danger got closer.

She moved behind the tree that they were resting under so she could have the intruders in her sight before they could see her.

Georgia watched as a woman appeared, carrying a bundle tied across one shoulder, then two men, one the size of Franklin and just as dark and the other a young man—a boy, she could see, as they stepped closer.

"Stop!" Georgia commanded in her deepest man-voice.

The travelers froze, as a deer does when they catch your scent or their finely honed ears hear you breathe.

She stuck her face partway around the tree, "What're you folks doin' here in the middle of the night with no torches to see with?"

The large man spoke. "What 're *you* doin' here in the middle of the night with no campfire, tent or lean-to?"

Hearing the man answer, Ebony peeked through a thin veil of blanket at their visitors and jumped up, revealing herself.

"What the ...?" The man was completely surprised at the sudden appearance of the girl.

Georgia stepped out from the tree, still holding the pistol on the three strangers. "Ebony, what are you ...?"

"These people are escaping their masters," Ebony said and she stood in front of the woman carrying the bundle. "We have to help them."

"We can't help ... we don't even know ..." A long pause. "... anything about where we are, who to trust, how to survive out here. That's why I was saying we should get on a northbound boat and skedaddle."

The man chimed in. "You can take us on the boat like we were your servants. You don't have to pay our fare, since we aren't 'people,' and they will expect us to work if they need extra hands."

"Do I look like I could own ... one, two, three, *four* servants?"

Her man-clothes were unwashed and a bit ragged around the edges. Her hair was knotted and quite unkempt.

They all saw that she was right and that the idea wouldn't

work. Each one sat down on a log or rock, looking disappointed, except Ebony. When she spoke, people listened.

"When the men are loading, there is a lot of confusion, and to the white people, especially the men in charge of the loading, we all look alike. Papa and I found families hiding among the passengers sometimes. You just can't stay on too long, because the other workers can get mean and point you out."

Georgia looked at the collection of humanity and tried to decide which ones she might be able to 'claim' as her 'servants.' Ebony was a given and would stick to her side like a tree frog to the skin of cypress tree.

It was not feasible for her to be in 'possession' of the large man under any circumstances. He read her dismay and said, "I think I can fool a fool. Don't worry about me. By the way, my name is Nathaniel. The boy here is Jacob and the woman is Prudence Red Hawk. Her mother was Cherokee and her husband was my brother. When he died two weeks ago, I promised him I'd take his wife to freedom. Jacob came along by accident."

A stunned expression formed on Georgia's face. "Well ... I ... I never met anyone besides me that was from two different blood lines. And it sure is a pleasure. I'm glad we came upon one another— all of us."

The next morning they shared provisions and headed toward the river. Georgia and Ebony led the way and the others trailed far behind until they reached the crowded docking packets.

They merged among the crowd invisibly like spies and milled about. Nathaniel picked up a wheelbarrow full of wood and boarded a boat. Prudence walked closely beside a lady in a fancy dress and feathered hat, as though she belonged to her, and boarded the same boat. Jacob was very late in catching up with them, but he made it onboard by standing around near the boat. When it came time to shove off, a steward shouted at him to "get his lazy so-and-so-self onboard."

Once aboard there were many ways to survive, and they even felt a little safe. Georgia and Ebony shared a cabin with the cook in exchange for washing potatoes and dishes. There was a team of

Swedish dishwashers on board; having extra help meant much needed down-time for them, which they spent learning English.

Nathaniel met some other people headed for the Underground Railroad who told him the best place to disembark—or swim off at night.

"There might be patrols," they said, "but our people will be there to claim you are their property and take you away safely."

As it turned out, swimming was exactly what he and Prudence had to do. Georgia kept watch at the rail for the calmest, shallowest-looking spot and gave the go signal when those conditions were met *and* when no one was looking.

Nathaniel and Prudence made it to the other side, but Georgia heard hounds baying not far from where they landed. There was no way of knowing if they were safe or not. The dogs routinely patrolled by the river looking to capture escaping slaves.

Jacob took a liking to Ebony and felt protective of her. He really didn't trust Georgia to do the best for the child. For seventeen years he had lived in slave quarters, never allowed within fifty yards of the house for fear he might lay eyes on the daughters of his owner. The master's wife came to the shack one day where he and eight others lived and just took a girl much like Ebony, only eight, 'to teach her how to be a good maid.'

His voice quivered slightly as he told Ebony, "The girl's mother pleaded with the woman that her child was too young to be taken. The mama might as well have been the wind. That lady took the girl and no one ever saw her again." Jacob's only interaction with a white woman was with her being a kidnapper. Even though Georgia was only part white, he feared the same for this child.

It took seven more days to get to Illinois. One of those days was the 4th of July. The shorelines were crowded in places with bands playing. They passed the same scene all day and all night. When night did come, fireworks sprouted and sprayed over the tops of the trees, lighting up church spires and picket fences. The boat was a more dangerous place to be that night for all the drinking and gunfire. Flashes from hot gunpowder lit up bushy-bearded faces and stoic gentlemen standing nearby. The water reflected the bursting lights in the sky and rippled them back to the shore.

It was exhilarating and nerve-wracking and cruelly ironic for Georgia, Ebony and the other remaining Negroes. Such noises would be expected if they were to be hunted or found out. Celebration of 'freedom' was not a reality for any of them. They comforted each other and were glad to be leaving the next day.

Less than a handful of people got off in Illinois at the Troy, stopping point. That caused the next group of fugitives to stand out and the risk of being caught was making all three of them nervous, just when they thought they would be the safest.

Jacob was to wait until the very last minute before trying to slip off without being seen.

There were only a few bags of corn being loaded and the loadmaster was being very picky about how he wanted them handled and where they were to be put. He stood at the gangway shouting, "Move that trunk over there. Keep that cotton dry. Watch what you're doin', you're gonna topple that stack," and other commands until the plank was lifted and the ropes were hauled on board.

A split second after the loadmaster turned his back and took a step away from the side of the boat, Jacob moved like a blur behind him and splashed through two feet of water to get to dry ground. He made it to shore, but Georgia lost sight of him after that.

She imagined him as a young Wade, getting along and doing all right. Then she thought of him as Franklin, with his deep distrust and quick temper. But he had had Nathaniel for a guide and mentor, too; maybe that would be how he would grow up. She wished him well as he disappeared to meet his own destiny.

Because Georgia and Ebony had boarded as a woman and her servant, there was nothing odd about their exit together. Georgia took Ebony on her shoulders and tossed a bundle with foodstuffs and an extra blanket up to Ebony, who put it on her head. They looked like one very tall, graceful African woman taking the laundry to be washed.

Fourteen

Family Isn't Always Blood

It took a day or two before they were convinced they were in 'safe' territory for Ebony. Georgia was never 'safe', not here, in the North. All her troubles began in northern territory. She had enough coins to coax a stage driver to let them ride, but the rest stop wouldn't take Georgia's money, assuming she had stolen it from white people. So, even though they had the luxury of riding during the day, they were once again forced to sleep outside on the ground at night. Hopefully it would be their last night out on the ground, since the coachman had told them they were only a day away from Midlothian by foot.

Ebony started singing in the morning like she had heard the birds and when they began, she stopped singing to listen. The girls' spirits rose to match the lightness that comes with birdsong. Their steps were quick and rhythmic and sped up to a trot.

An old Indian peered out from the woods. His clothing matched the color of the trunks of the trees. It made him invisible.

Georgia's spirits were high and she announced, "We're coming to civilization. Look! A picket fence up there and the well-traveled road."

No sooner had Georgia uttered the words than the rumbling, jingling, clatter of a stagecoach, charging full speed, arose behind them. They stood aside and watched it fly by. The driver's grizzled beard divided perfectly down the middle and pressed back to his ears against the wind. He was smiling from ear to ear, and if they could have, Georgia thought the horses would have been smiling, too.

"That driver and those horses are heading for the barn," Georgia said.

Lots of new buildings were going up and she knew that Harley was connected to all that. He had been the supervisor when the barn at her house was built and did a good job at that.

After asking a few townsfolk, "Where does the carpenter live? His wife is Clara," they found Aunt Clara's house, at last. Georgia thought the hug Clara gave her would never end, but she couldn't squirm out of it. Instead, she broke the clench by squeezing out the words. "This is Ebony. She needs a family."

Georgia saw the shocked expression on Clara's face when she realized that Ebony was with Georgia and not a local waif. "Oh, dear Lord, No!" Clara whispered. Georgia was surprised at that reaction coming from Clara.

"I thought this was a free state. The Negroes on the boat said the Underground Railroad was thriving here," Georgia said.

"All that is true, but not everyone who lives here is in accordance with that. You well know your Uncle Harley's attitude. We'll have to find a way to ease Ebony into the house. Harley won't abide having both of you here or Ebony *in* our house, at least not without a strong argument." Clara was snuggling Ebony next to her waist to reassure her of her own feelings.

"I'm so sorry darlin'," Georgia explained, "but he's a very difficult man. He's like the cargo boss on the boat."

"What can we do, Aunt Clara?" Georgia replied. "You don't have a barn or even an attic we can put her in."

"I think I have a place in the house. We'll have her stay in hiding until I can tell him about her and assure him it'll only be for a few days at most. That will give me time to find a family for her. I think I know of one now, but I'll ask them tomorrow. We can't just set her on their doorstep today."

With the circumstances settled and understood, Clara took them inside for rabbit stew, bread and tea. She explained, "Harley will be at work until sundown or after. The town is growing fast and he and a crew are putting up buildings on the main street, with a promise of building the church after that."

Clara made Ebony comfortable in an alcove where the bedding was kept. Harley never bothered with such things. Even though it was right under his nose, he would never look in there for anything. Clara made a thick padding of sheets and blankets for a mattress and covered Ebony with a quilt.

"Thank you, ma'am. I don't want to cause any sort of trouble for you. I really don't. If I do, you just send me somewhere else." Ebony's sincerity was clear. "It'll be all right, Ebony", Clara said, "I have ways with my man. And we will find you a Negro family as soon as possible." Aunt Clara's tone was reassuring. Ebony was asleep the moment she closed her eyes.

Georgia was outside watching birds line up on the roof of the neighbor's house to face the sun. She once told Wade, "I believe that they sing the sun up in the morning and every sundown they honor the power that provided them with everything they needed that day. She joined them and let her spirit feel the fullness of gratitude for being safe at Clara's, and getting Ebony to a safe place. The God that white men said they followed was not in her thoughts. The God that cared for the birds and Ebony *was* in her heart. She had no name for such a god and no rituals or dogma to maintain, but the mysterious ways of an unseen power kept her curious and alive.

When Ebony sank into her deep sleep, Georgia and Clara talked for hours.

"What happened over there at the farm?" Clara asked. "Who could have done such a thing?" Georgia recalled the letter she sent and realized there had been no mention as to why the horrible things had happened. Her main objective had been to inform and, most of all, to warn Clara not to come.

"The killers said some Indians wiped out a family and left the oldest girl alive. So they came to do the same to me." Her voice and demeanor were pensive and distant. Clara was stunned, speechless. Silence lay heavy between them and then they both spoke at once, running over each other's words. "I can't fathom anyone doing..." Clara started to say.

"It was church people. I recognized the voice of one and the horses of most of the rest." Her anger was rising and so was her tone.

Clara stopped to listen.

"No one came afterward," Georgia said, "not even Orville."

"Oh, you dear child!" said Clara, beginning to weep. "How did you manage? Where did you go?"

Georgia told her about staying in the woods near the house

and scavenging things from it to trade. She told of her adventures on the boat, the tragedy of losing Huck; the farms she had worked and how she and Ebony got together. Speaking of the horrors brought back the hatred she had set aside so many times. All tenderness was forgotten now.

All the while Clara listened without interrupting. Compassion was written on her face in the tears rolling down her cheeks.

When Georgia finished, Clara asked, "What in the world will you do now?"

Georgia thought for a while and said with a chuckle and a hint of sarcasm, "God only knows."

Clara smiled briefly then a veil of seriousness dropped over her from head to toe. "Despite what the 'church people' did, God has been in charge of your life from the time you were conceived, your birth and, odd as it may seem, even now." The tone in her voice didn't even seem like Clara's.

She went on. "November 10, 1833, the night before you were born, there were so many stars falling from the sky, it was nearly like daylight. Your mother went into labor as the sun was setting the following day and the stars fell again that night—at least as many and maybe more. Such events don't come along very often and you being born on that night confirmed Julia's belief that your conception was part of a greater destiny." Georgia listened in stunned silence.

"Something else. Every year at the same time for the past seventeen years, it happens again," Clara said.

"Mother told me about Blue Stone being my father of seed," Georgia said. "She didn't seem to know much about him other than he was a Sioux, his name was Blue Stone, and she *said* she loved him."

"She did love him, and he loved her. He risked his life just by helping her, and when Uncle Jake and Grandpa found him with her in the shelter he built, they would have killed him, but he wouldn't leave her and your mother stood in front of him and talked them down."

Georgia shook her head and stood up arrow straight. "I can't believe that. What I *do* believe is she only did that because she was kind and didn't want to watch them kill him. I know she said it all seemed like 'destiny,' but she could have thought and said that, even if he had forced himself on her. People lie to themselves all the time. She was protecting her dignity."

Clara stepped closer and countered. "Things happen to people—between people, sometimes—that no one can explain. Things may happen to you that seem to have been planned without your knowledge, things that have put you in a certain place at a certain time for an unknown reason. That place and that time are like a gift devised for you and whoever might be there with you. And the nature of the gift and the timing of it are too perfect to be ignored."

Georgia thought of the hawk, the dream, and the perfection of the realization of that dream and Ebony's words that Georgia was a gift to her.

Clara continued. "If Blue Stone had forced himself on her, why would she stand out in all kinds of weather staring at the horizon, hoping for a glimpse of him or a message from him? If he had forced himself on her, why would she have kept you and loved you and found a man that could love you, too? She could have sent you back to the tribe ... or worse."

Georgia had no answer and had much to think about. She dropped her head and stared at the floor.

Clara went on. "I began by telling you that God is very much in charge of your life. I believe that for many reasons, but the most important is this: you have been given qualities that can bring the white man and Indian together. You have been given courage, wisdom, and stamina to use for the benefit of others. But if you choose to use those attributes for revenge or hatred, they will devour you and give you a miserable and, possibly brief, life."

Clara looked deep into Georgia's eyes and held that gaze until she was certain her words had found fertile ground. She went on. "Something else you really need to know. I have heard from a very reliable source that Blue Stone is considered a holy man in his tribe. He is not a warrior or murderer of white people. Indians revere him and so do whites that get to know him. That is partially due to having saved your mother's life ... and others, as well. I think you should learn more about your Indian heritage and seek him out to see for yourself what kind of man he is."

Georgia scowled at first then slowly let the words soften her attitude. "How do you know all this?" she asked. "Have you ever met him?"

"Call it providence, or coincidence, but a woman from his tribe brings a group of women ..."

"What? How did the tribe get over the river? Georgia said, "Why would they come here anyway?"

"The women help thresh the wheat in the fall. One has learned some English over the years and a white man with her tribe interpreted for us last year to confirm that we understood her."

Georgia tried to unravel the knots in her midsection and quiet the angry voices rebelling at every word Clara was saying. Suddenly the square rooms of the house were much too confining. She had to go outside.

The moon had a tinge of blue and its look of surprise made her think, *you've seen all this and more. Are you still surprised at what humans do?* Clara had made some convincing points about God being in charge, but why He would take her family so violently, and subject her to the hatred that hounded her, was still a mystery to her. For the time being it would remain a mystery. The basis for all human curiosity—what is on the other side of that hill, or ocean, or mountain—was built into her through her heritage, and it was pushing and pulling her to find out what was ahead and unravel the mystery.

Even though Clara's house was nestled between two others— a crowded neighborhood, to Georgia—the animal inhabitants still claimed the area. A wolf sent one long, mournful greeting to the night, the moon, and Georgia. She closed her eyes, let her ears inhale the wolf's chant into her skin, and stood reverently as one who is deep in prayer stays silent until the prayer drifts off. Georgia absorbed every nuance of the wolf's plea and went back into the house.

Over the next few days, Ebony was settled quickly and Harley did pitch a major fit, but it became clear he was going to have to accept the idea. However, it was easy for him to give up a horse to Georgia just to be rid of her. Clara promised to find Ebony another place soon and Harley sulked but didn't argue, as Clara's word was her bond.

Georgia struggled with the thought of leaving Ebony or taking her along. Thoughts of what responses they would attract, a Negro child and a half-breed Indian, sealed her conclusion. Ebony, at least, would be better off here, and Clara had convinced everyone she could find a family to take her in, while Clara would become her teacher.

Georgia had saddlebags packed with supplies and her journal and took her time patting it down and adjusting the reins. When nothing more could be done, the moment she had been dreading was clearly present. She crouched near the child and they pressed their cheeks together each looking forward not at each other. They spent many moments in silent communication. Ebony's parting words to Georgia were, "Go with God." Georgia hugged her firmly and turned away.

Clara tenderly stroked the white streak in Georgia's hair, as Julia used to do, and made her promise to write.

It was hard to say goodbye to Ebony and Clara, but Georgia decided that she had enough sadness and was happy to be riding free again. The last thing she said to Clara before riding off was, "I would really like to see the city of Savannah. If I get there, maybe then I will go look for Blue Stone."

Clara warned as Georgia turned the horse hard. "We heard last week, Blue Stone is moving the whole tribe south and west. He had a vision that told him to move there. You may not find him if you go to Savannah first."

Georgia had a lot to think about: whether to go back to the McDaniel's farm or find Blue Stone; whether to ride the Mississippi south to see Savannah; or go west where all those wagons were headed. Then the smell of the leather saddle, the sweat of the horse, and a tinge of smoke in the wind reminded her of where she was right now. Free to meet the challenges of whatever faced her, free to fight them or accept them. Free to learn what was best. Free to *be*.

At the edge of town, a gust of wind took her hat off; the drawstring pressed hard into her neck. With the hat laying between her shoulders and the streak of white gleaming in the sunlight, she passed an Indian woman on the road. The woman saw the white streak in her hair and knew. When she returned to her village, she told the others she had seen Blue Stone in the form of a woman, riding south. The chief sent two warriors to follow.

Fifteen

Webster Searches Far and Wide

Webster discovered that the nearest town of any size west of the Mississippi was several days' ride from the trading post. But he made his way across the Big River to Midlothian and found many Clara's in the town. However, no girl to fit that description had been seen.

He stayed near the shore watching the steamboats in Troy, a few days after the 4th of July. A saloon girl told him about a young woman that she thought was Negro adopting an orphaned Negro child. Webster dismissed it, deciding it couldn't be Savannah. He traced a path from Midlothian to St. Louis riding up and down the river and looking in towns near the river – he had no sight of her and no one else did either.

During this time, Blue Stone had moved the tribe across the river and further south.

Several times in Webster's search, he came near to death and each time someone or some *thing* came to his rescue. Even rain. A time that thirst so severe his tongue swelled out of his mouth caused him to pass out. He fell on his back. It began to rain so hard he thought he would drown as water poured into his open cavern. Once, he was attacked by a small band of renegade Crow. The stone that Blue Stone gave him fell out of his pocket and the attackers froze in position, suddenly halted their assault and turned and rode off.

He felt it may have been a signal to find Blue Stone, even though he had not achieved the goal, he stayed with his clan, interpreting English and learning a bit of Lakota. Fixing misunderstandings and learning more about self-sufficiency from the tribe kept him busy enough not to notice the time that slipped past.

News that his people were engaged in a war over slavery and whether or not to continue the practice moved him to help in any way he could.

When he approached Blue Stone, the same feeling he had leaving his father and brother welled up inside. *How can I disappoint this man again? I failed in finding his daughter and he welcomed me and cared for me like a son. He always defends me to other Indians. How can I do this?*

Blue Stone had also heard of the war in the invading culture. He knew the moment he heard the news that Webster would be seeking a way to bring justice to the laws of his people.

Blue Stone stood with his arms wide open for the whole time it took Webster to walk the length of the camp. Each step brought a stronger knowing that Blue Stone understood.

Webster fell into that embrace. They looked each other in the eyes with their arms clasped in the Indian way and then Webster walked away.

Maybe if I work near the river, I can still find her. He thought as he rode off.

Troy had a stagecoach manufacturer that hired him He learned quickly. Driving, building, repairing the stagecoaches came easily for him.

One day while he was resting out back of his workplace, Georgia rode by the front, wearing trousers and her hat covering her hair. No one even noticed she was female.

When he went back to work and entered through the front door, she was gone and she never came that close again.

Sixteen

When Georgia Turned Twenty-One

The McDaniels' farm looked very different at the end of summer than it had in the spring years before. Green and gold from corn and wheat filled the landscape from horizon to horizon

Georgia had been away for over three years. She was twenty-one now and had fought most of her demons into submission. The city of Savannah had been a disappointment and survival had kept her from searching for her father. There were some circumstances that triggered a knee-jerk angry response. But rages were few. She was proud to have overcome them.

Chickens making their wary, long-winded noises, coupled with the familiar scenery and smells, enwrapped her senses. No other place could be home like this place.

She rode up to the house, which had been painted pastel lavender, and called to the house. "Hello! Who's home? Ruth? Wade?"

A large-boned woman opened the door and stood as though guarding the house from pillagers. Her arms were crossed and her right hand was waggling a very large rolling pin. Her frame took up nearly all the space in the doorway. "Who would ya be, now? And what you want with those that ain't here?"

"I'm ... I worked here a couple of years ago and the missus—Missus McDaniels—told me to come back whenever I wanted."

"That don't tell me a thing about who you are. You look Injun, but you talk as good as a white. Which are ya, then?"

Georgia noticed a hint of Irish, like her own mother's, in the woman's speech. It was pleasant to hear it again and made her smile "My name is Georgia Dunbar. My father is Sioux and my dearly departed mother was Irish."

With a total change in demeanor the woman said, "Well, well, well, come on in. I think Missus McDaniels spoke about you. Wasn't that you nearly froze to death in a spring snow? Won't you have some tea?"

"Now you know who I am ... who would you be?" Georgia was playfully imitating the Irish lilt.

"Name is Sally O' Connor. I take care of the farm hands and the house for Ruth. Gavin, that's Mister McDaniels, is my cousin. I came up from Missouri to keep the place for them."

"Where ... are they ...?"

"No, child. They're alive and kicking up their heels somewhere called San Francisco in California. He sent for her to come see all the wonders there are in that place."

"Wonders?"

"Oh, they have opera and an ocean and trolleys. She wrote and said they have gardens and museums with objects from all corners of the globe."

Georgia was stunned. She had never heard of opera but at least she knew what an ocean looked like. And trolleys.

"Well, where's Wade? Is he all right?"

"He got a visit from his dear mother. They went up to some big city where she lives so she could show him all that she wants to leave him when she passes. He should be back soon for the harvest. It's gonna be a big one."

"His mother? How did she find him?"

"Don't know. Could have been sheer luck, I guess. I didn't ask. He didn't seem to want to say, either."

Georgia had finished her tea and now she sat the cup down. "Thanks for the tea," she said. "What's the bunking situation? Are there quarters for me anywhere—away from the men?"

"Well, there's the loft here in the house. We don't have women..."

"I know. The loft will do fine, if you don't mind the intrusion."

"Say! Why don't I take the loft and you stay down here? I like how warm it is up there and this feather bed come all the way from Ireland. Try it out."

"I'm not used to soft … especially … really soft beds. But, since you're willing, I'll give it a try for a few nights. I didn't even ask if you need any help. There's a lot I can do. I can help with canning, shucking, cutting, laundry … but I'm not a very good cook."

"We'll use you as an all-around helper, and don't you worry. They send plenty of money to use for emergencies and extra hands and my pies have won a few blue ribbons at the fair. I'll be doin' the cookin' and bakin'."

"I thank you for your hospitality." Georgia said, "There's a lot of daylight left and I have an important stop to make." With that, she rode off to the meadow past the pond. Sprinklings of sparkles caught her eye as dragonfly wings glittered on nearly every leaf of the cattails. A few geese had joined the ducks in the pond and the sight made her feel that much more at home.

Harley was not in his perch in the meadow or anywhere else on the farm. There were hawks surfing the skies and calling to their mates, but no amount of coaxing or prime meat offerings could bring them to her arm.

Some days she tried several times. There were no takers, no Harley, and no replacements. Each fruitless effort added to her let-down as the days went by with no trace of her friend.

The numbers of hawks increased for a week or two and she realized they were migrating, but there was no Harley among them, either. Long after the migration was over, she resigned not to search for him anymore.

One evening, during her ride to commune she noticed a few stars blink in the pinkish sky. A figure came riding. She watched them approach from a distance of over mile. Closer range helped her vision focus on the size and shape of the rider. Her curiosity outdid her annoyance at the intrusion and she sat in the same spot while the man aboard came into view.

"Wade!" She shouted, as she waved her hat and stood up in the stirrups.

The horseman sped up his mount and she could see his teeth in contrast to his dark clothes and skin.

"Wade!" She called again spurring her horse to meet him.

Disbelieving his own eyes and ears, he asked, "Georgia?"

They met in the middle of the road and each dismounted and flung into each others arms, laughing and stumbling, and slapping backs simultaneously.

"You almost missed the harvest you ol' owl, but I'm sure glad you made it." She said.

"If I'd known you were here, I'd been here a week ago. Come tell me your adventures and I'll tell you mine." His snowy beard was a testament to the time that had passed. Wade was beaming broadly as they rode side by side back to the house.

Harvest was accomplished with the help of the neighbors and all of their hired hands. It had only taken three weeks because of all the machinery and because neighbors shared equipment and hired hands to get it all in.

Hard work behind them, they could now celebrate. Fiddles and washboards, stomping feet and the clapping of wooden spoons took their spirits away from their calloused and bleeding hands, their too-tanned faces and their aching backs. Georgia hadn't seen so much food in one place since Phineas' wake. Children ran all about chasing the dogs, winding under arched arms and through the bowed legs of the dancers, and dodging boot heels.

All too soon the day's fun ended and, finally, when there was nothing left to be done. Sally asked her to stay over and help with the canning, reminding Georgia that she had mentioned it when she arrived. Sally didn't think Georgia would stay—she knew Georgia would want some solitude—out with the earth and sky, wind and weather. Which is why she was surprised when Georgia said, "I consider that a promise and I will stay until the spirit moves me to travel on."

Before supper that night Georgia went out to breathe the crisp evening air for a while. Waves of birds were declaring their winter warnings—those sounds that spur people below to prepare for their own hibernation.

We follow the example of the tribal people who listen to the call of the birds.

Georgia listened to the calls and responses, she thought that she ought to know what they were saying, but the language was long lost, hidden deep in layers of history. She couldn't make out the words, but the tones and the timing were familiar. Nonetheless, as the birds passed overhead in the dusty orange sky, she stood transfixed in the yard and bid each flock a good journey. No one else ever did that or told her to do it—it just seemed natural.

As dusk brought out the first stars, Georgia clasped her shawl around her, grasped her shoulders, hugged herself in reassurance that she would survive the winter, and returned to the house.

Peering through the window before she went back inside, she saw Sally dipping into the steaming pots on the Behemoth—as Missus called her enormous stove. The windows were teary with moisture and Sally's curls wept over her ears. Several large pots of boiling water filled with the men's clothes, or sheets, or potatoes, covered the top of the beast front and back and side to side.

That routine went on for weeks with all the chores and meals occurring like clockwork.

Suppertime routine mimicked morning, with Sally orbiting around and around the table, ladling out soup in one orbit, then potatoes, then chunks of meat, laughing and joking with the rowdy bunch of hungry men as she dished out the food.

Harvey, the thinnest of the bunch, complained, as usual. "C'mon, Sally," he said, spreading his arms, exposing his stick-like frame. "Can't you see I need more than that paltry pile of potatoes hand 'em over?"

"To be sure," said Sally, "I do know that pitiful patch of potatoes will not fill your hollow leg, but if you recall, the last time I let you piglets help yourself, I had to replace lamps and chairs – AND it took me and Georgia days to clean the floors and walls from you fools fightin' over the scraps."

Some of the men grinned; some hung their heads.

"Just a bunch of rowdy little boys, rasselin' like you don't know any better." The curls framing her face bounced and bobbed with her laughter as she shook her wooden spoon at those seated at the table.

Sally was easy to laugh and it looked good on her round

cheeks and big-boned frame. No children of her own, but she was good at mothering the ragged bunch collected at her table. Taking turns teasing and being teased, and she didn't mind mild swearing. But if a ruffian got out of hand with it, she would tap on his noggin with that spoon—that was all it took.

Thirty years ago Sally had been the only survivor of a wagon train raided by bandits on the Oregon Trail. Now, in her forties, she'd buried the spouses and children of many neighbors and travelers. In spite of all the misery life handed her, she reminded Georgia of Ebony.

"Everything is in God's hands," she'd always say when reminded of her troubles.

Those words were the one thing that still got Georgia riled. "That outlaw scum who stole your family's provisions and ultimately caused the death of your younger sister and both your parents weren't doin' God's work." She took a breath. "God, as you call it, didn't show that He cared one twit for me. He left my father under his horse that had a broken leg until they were both dead." Georgia was letting it all spill out to one she knew could understand.

Sally listened as the girl went on.

"Men who went to church every Sunday took the life of my little brother and my mother before my eyes and burnt our farm to the ground a week after I turned eighteen and I've been struggling to survive ever since."

Georgia was not in the habit of expressing her feelings about God and she stopped herself now. When she trusted someone enough to tell anything about herself, she usually told stories of her adventures steering clear of the painful parts of her history.

Sally's face softened and she slowly moved her head back in forth as if in disbelief. "God knew what kind of life He had in mind for each and every one of us and did it His way. I may never know why he spared me, and it's pointless to question Him and His doin's, but you go right ahead. He gave us all a lifetime to learn in."

Sally let the moment ease into comfortable silence and then she said, "I knew when you came here you had no place to call home, and it's plain to see you're not ready to settle. You'll do all right with your wrangling and such, but sooner or later you'll see that you're only slightly in charge of your own life and the reason you have survived is because a greater spirit is watching out for you. C'mon now, let's get those clothes wrung out."

The two women went back to work. Two rods were wrapped with a piece of damp clothing. Sally held one and Georgia held the other. Twisting each one to wring it as dry as they could, then hanging it on a line that zig-zagged through the wide open room, made the house cozier than before.

Sally and Georgia moved through their chores as though choreographed by an expert. Dishes clanked and clattered as they worked their well-rehearsed dance to clean, dry, and set them up for the morning. Sally's evening ritual was to untie her apron with a flourish, fold it over the banister, send up a satisfying sigh, and head up to her bed at the top of the stairs, saying "Night darlin'. Stay snug as a bug in a rug."

Seventeen

November 10, 1854

Her skin was still balmy from the sauna effect in the kitchen. Crisp, cold air met her exposed cheeks and eyes, instantly awakening the wandering spirit that urged her out the door.

The moment her foot touched the ground, Brother Wolf tipped his head back and released his devotional song to that same spirit. His pack family joined him then from all directions the call echoed around and within her.

In her heart she knew they were calling down a spirit army to run with them; to feel the glaze of the cold on their whiskers and the edges of their fur; calling them to come make little clouds with their breath, while their hot blood was cooled as they stamped their existence in the snow.

Suddenly, their chorus stopped. It took her breath away. A lonely owl punctuated the silence then his last mournful note drifted away on the wind.

She had given herself over to the sounds and senses with all the natural, innate feelings that arose. This was her spiritual place—outside: wind for music; water speaking with its many voices; thunder, the hooves of heaven; birds, animals speaking in their own tongues—this was her church.

The sight of her own visible breath propelled her thoughts to a clear mental image of her mother, standing at the fence line in crisp weather, and even darkest winter.

Mother was giving reverence, too—to a distant unknown, maybe a time and place. Why did I never ask what you were looking for, praying for?

She felt the absence of her mother with deep regret and hung her head for a moment.

Something caught her eye. She raised her head to see three stars fall at once. The sky began to fall.

A handful of stars slipped behind the house. She took a few steps and a dozen more fell, all at once. She turned around with her head tilted back and watched a hoard of lights glide out of the heavens.

She stood awestruck, drinking it all in.

Yelps, whoops and drums from a nearby encampment of Indians woke the farm hands and Sally who came down the stairs. The first thing she noticed was an empty bed.

Sally to called for her in a perfect pitch, high C note. "Georrrrrrrrrgiaaaaaa!"

Stars were streaking by the hundreds or thousands and lit the sky from horizon to horizon.

"I'm all right, Sally. It's my birthday, the stars are falling."

The Indian drums beat like hearts imbued with fear or passion, which awakened the farmhands in a fight-or-flight state of mind and body. Georgia hoped good sense would keep this perfect night from turning violent.

The farm hands had scrambled to their horses and were in the process of bridling and saddling them when Frank put it all together. "Never mind, boys. They're drumming to the sky god or something to do with the falling stars. Back to bed with ya."

Later, back in her room, Georgia stroked the cover of her journal as she thought of Aunt Clara and Ebony before writing in it for a few moments. Then she pulled back the lace curtain Mrs. Ruth had sent, snuggled into her down cover, and watched the falling stars until she fell into a peaceful sleep.

Eighteen

Spring of 1856

Every year, after the planting and the spring birthing of calves, lambs, foals, and chicks were done, Georgia rode off for solitude and rebonding with her most natural self.

Mr. Croft, a neighbor, knew of this habit and watched her work to a full sweat in the fall harvesting and during these arduous spring exertions. He had three stocky sons to help him and he brought them all to help at the McDaniels' when Sally was short of hands.

Georgia saw him smiling at her several times then looking away quickly when she caught him.

Even though she felt uneasy when the effects of his gaze caused her to turn and see him staring, she felt worse when he would turn away quickly. It seemed another example of people not wanting to see her around.

I wonder what he's planning, she thought and cringed as she remembered the man-boy.

During the spring shindig, Mr. Croft was more conspicuous by his absence. Georgia hid out as usual, feigning to look after all the newborn critters, now fully capable of survival. She puttered around in the barn and chatted with the chickens and cats, content to be among animal life.

Hoof beats caught her attention, and then one of the younger Croft boys ran into the barn yelling, "Georgia! Georgia! Come look!"

Not inclined to move at someone else's demand, she finished scooping a corner of a stall and nonchalantly put her gloves in her pockets, carefully put the shovel on a hook, dusted off her pant legs and moseyed over to see what the ruckus was about.

The older Croft boy was sitting atop a large, white stallion whose coat and mane were as white as the streak in her hair. The boy glided down the side of the horse and handed her the rope he used as a rein to guide it.

"S' name's Moonshine. Father thought you should have him." He could barely be heard. She read in his voice, and in his general demeanor, that he had probably been expecting to have this wonderful creature for his own.

Dumbfounded by such a gift, a long silence went by while she choked down her overwhelming gratitude. She swallowed the lump in her throat several times before she was able to finally say a heartfelt, "Thank you. Tell your father …" The word father triggered the lump back into her throat, larger than the last time.

Nothing more came from her lips. The boys were so uncomfortable they went off, kicking dirt clods and shoving each other as they meandered home.

She petted the velvety snout of her new friend and gazed deep into his eyes.

He ruffed gently and even more tenderly petted her ear with his soft nostril. Then, with no bridle, blanket, saddle or reins, she leapt up on him and they flew like the wind. It was understood, as if they had been together for years that he was to take her wherever his massive heart wished.

Only the rope he came with connected them physically. Yet, somehow, Georgia knew the big stallion knew her heart as well as his own, and he took her far from farms and houses and horses. Far from words and eyes that speak.

They rode until the light of the sun gave way to moonlight that made his white coat glow like silver.

He stopped by a stream where she could hear the splash of fish grabbing an evening meal and watch a few of the first fireflies rise from invisibility and speak their love songs with their light.

Moonshine drank his fill from the stream and she rubbed him down with her work-worn hands, each stroke reaffirming the love and trust between them.

When they had both rested, she climbed up on his back, and

again, their understanding was mutual. He walked most of the way back and they enjoyed the air, glittering fire flies, the stars, and each other's company as long as they could.

Spring of 1856 brought a chain of events that eluded her normally prophetic dreams. Word had it that a new army outpost had been built fifty miles as the crow flies from the farm. Rumors swirled about its purpose, who was in charge, and how the nearest town was overrunning with soldier's money after a payday.

Curiosity burned in her brain like money in her pocket. The alleged activity was in the opposite direction from where she and Moonshine usually rode. However, the thought of new territory spurred her on more. Not knowing the area well, she packed extra rations and a bigger bedroll in case weather was harsh.

A fifty-mile difference could bring any number of surprises. "Sorry ol' bud, if this is too much for ya," she teased. Moonshine was in his prime and as sturdy as a plow horse, but lean and long on endurance. He turned his head to read her eyes, as if trying to determine if that was a joke. It was. He snorted, hard.

Among the extras she took this time were her diary and a pencil. Winters, with their moody, dark, early hush, were more conducive to writing. But this spring, inspiration spilled out and awakened the writing muse. She managed a letter to Clara and Ebony describing her marvelous steed. Ebony had been writing back to show how much she had learned. Clara kept her informed about the growth of the town and wishes for her to join them in winter's dreadful span. The perfect weather inspired Georgia to write longer than usual, but back on the horse she leapt.

At the end of a lovely ride, through meadows of wildflowers surrounded by hedgerows of wild roses, she could write to her heart's content.

"Look, my friend! Hills! With nice big oaks, with tall grasses around them and shade underneath. You go eat, I'm going exploring."

The oaks sat at the top of a rise, blocking the view beyond it. Moonshine's munching and the twittering of a few birds were the only sounds, and the aroma of the crushed grass as she waded through it even smelled green renewing her bond to untamed earth.

Over the rise lay a wide expanse littered with bodies whose limbs and heads lay scattered haphazardly. It looked like something wild had charged through a rendering plant made for human beings.

A closer look revealed the contents of sleeves, pant legs, and neck holes, spilling something other than flesh and blood.

She tiptoed forward, scanning the scene and trying to make sense of it.

"Scarecrows! Ha! Practice bodies for battle." Her exclamation startled a batch of crows dining on some real carrion. She chided the bodies, "You guys aren't very good scarecrows."

The fifteen horse lengths between her and the crow fest were too close for them and they lifted off in a variety of crackles and cackles. All but one and it wasn't a crow. It stood head and shoulders above the others when they were gathered around.

"Why didn't you fly, big fella?"

The bird raised its wings the best it could, but one hung awkwardly down.

She stepped closer, very slowly, and cautiously.

The years had flown by and she had been reluctant to seek out her hawk in the meadow by the pond. Knowing that wild things are better kept as wild as possible, she told herself Harley the Hawk wouldn't miss her or know her, and the only reason he had come to her was for the delicious offerings she brought.

This bird made no attempt to hide or fight and it didn't attempt to escape since it couldn't fly. It looked at her, first with one eye and then the other. It opened its beak and squeaked out several short, high-pitched notes, then rocked back and forth almost hopping up and down.

"What? What's wrong now, then? The ground's not hot. Why are you so excited?"

The bird hopped around in a circle and she saw the missing tail feathers.

"Harley?"

He hopped onto her shoulder. She screamed in pain from his talons. He hopped off.

She scrambled around the field, looking for thicker material to shield her arms and shoulders. There was a leather vest and one pair of fancy, heavy leather gloves she scavanged from the dissembled scarecrows. Georgia pulled them on then went back to the bird.

Harley let her touch his wing as long as she needed. Her expert touch and experience with so many animals helped to determine it was not a broken bone but perhaps a pulled muscle or other sinew. Georgia was convinced; time would give him back his power of flight.

She hunted down a rabbit and shared it with Harley before placing him in the big oak to roost for the night, safe from other predators.

Helping Harley heal kept her at that site for a few days. One morning a rumbling woke her abruptly thinking it was thunder, she bolted out of her pallet, pulled on her clothes and rolled up her bedroll—just that fast. Only then did she realize it wasn't thunder but the rumbling of soldiers, wagons, horses and equipment come to disturb her reverie.

Quickly she coaxed Harley onto her arm and Moonshine was already out of sight, so all Georgia had to do now was gather up her bedroll and hide. There were many rock outcroppings to hide behind, but Harley was spooked by all the booming and smoke from the battle practice. It was hard to contain him without restraining him completely, and that would definitely not work. She found a small piece of leather to use for a hood, but she had to hold it on for hours until the soldiers left because they spent all day with their war games and rifle practice. She was hungry and very uncomfortable with only rocks to stretch out upon. Harley got the better part of what was left of the rabbit she had rolled into the blanket with everything else.

Only an hour or two of sun was left when the men finally rattled off to their fort.

The days crept by. Her restlessness was urging her to ride, but she wouldn't leave Harley and couldn't take him until she was certain he'd survive the journey and more. Several times she mounted Moonshine, fully intending to give him free rein and charge off. Each time, however, she remembered Harley saving her from the man-boy attacker years ago.

At dusk the rabbits came out to feed and she encouraged the bird to glide after them. His strength improved every couple of days, and after a few weeks, she woke to a horrible stench.

Harley had brought her breakfast. However, he never noticed that she didn't eat skunk.

She praised him for his efforts and offered the skunk to him. The skin was a perfect wrap for her arm to hold the bird and protect her skin. After wrapping the skunk skin around her arm, she held her arm up and Harley landed on it. She swept her arm upward and he moved both wings with equal strength and power.

"Hoooooorayyyyyy for Harley! Now we can go home!"

Golden morning sunlight tinted Moonshine's white coat with its glory. Georgia's fringes leapt wildly in the breeze, Harley sat majestically on her arm, and her steed reared back in his own exuberance to run.

"Home! Lead us home, Moonshine!"

Georgia had been gone past her usual spring jaunt by over a week and some days.

Sally and all the hands had been worried enough to send a few out looking for her. Work got behind, Sally was losing sleep and trying to keep up in the house.

Georgia's reception upon her return was nothing less than that given royalty entering the castle walls. All the hands rushed on horse and on foot to meet her. Sally rang the dinner bell to call them all in, and the dogs leapt and spun in circles of joy.

Harley was nervous, but she had put his hood on a few miles from the farm. When she removed it, he aimed for the top of the tree that housed the beehive and settled there.

Sally had lots of questions and Georgia had lots of stories. But their favorite, by far, was Harley's choice for Georgia's breakfast.

Exhaustion was reflected in Sally's face, and her shoulders drooped, Georgia found these attributes disturbing in this exceptionally strong woman she had come to admire. It brought pangs of guilt for her long absence, which had left more work for Sally.

Getting behind on a farm can be ruinous, and Georgia had to work almost doubly hard all spring and summer to keep up. There was no catching up until harvest was over. As Sally said, "A good crop can be a blessing and a curse. Too much of a good thing brings waste and decay."

Through grueling summer heat, a tornado, and nights battling bird-sized mosquitoes, Georgia longed for harvest to begin.

At the end of the harvest that year, Georgia made plans to leave. Many evening discussions took place with Sally in an effort to focus on the right goal, for the right reasons.

The deciding moment didn't come like a flash of lightening or blinding revelation. It came through arduous, circuitous debate. Discussions about the 'true character' of Blue Stone, whether or not God or some form of guardian angel watches over us, and why there is pain in the world.

Georgia's questions about whether or not Blue Stone was evil would bring this response from Sally: "What does it matter, now? If he had loved your mother then, would that make him good? If life has made him angry—and he would have plenty of reason to be—does that make him evil now? If his character is such that he could never commit such evil as you imagine, and his evil is only in your imagination, how will you know unless you find him to see for yourself?"

Georgia was silent for a long time. "It probably is not a good idea for me to try to see him with any hatred in me," she finally replied. "Wade thinks it will be a bad idea."

"How will you conquer that, my dear?"

"I don't know. Sometimes, when I feel totally safe and guided by that unseen force, there is no hatred in me."

"That's love. Love was caring for Harley, finding safety for Ebony, all your work here to keep this farm going and doing your part every day, befriending Wade—all that is love."

"Why don't I know that? Why can't I feel that? How do you 'feel' that?"

"Feeling it while it's happening may not be possible. Nevertheless, looking at the results, and recognizing your part in doing something good and honorable, opens a door to gratitude, which flows in two directions. You feel gratitude for the chance to be a part, and do your part, and the Father bestows mercy to you. Mercy that you know you don't deserve will bring you to your knees with humility and increase your gratitude from your core for being loved by Him and for just being alive."

"Are you saying ... I *have* to believe in God to feel that?"

"I really don't know. However, I know He believes in you and will help you in ways you may never understand as long as you are in this world, because He already has. Take that for what it is worth to you."

Those words didn't seem to be coming from Sally. Georgia noticed there was a different tone in her voice and an unmistakable reflection of pure love in her countenance when she spoke them. The spirit that spoke through Clara and Ebony had reached Georgia again.

Sally rose from her chair, took off her apron with less flourish than usual, hung it on the railing, and headed up the stairs. "Night darlin', sleep tight, don't let the bedbugs bite." Her usual sigh was missing, and instead, she groaned a long moan when she reached the top of the stairs.

Georgia's routine was to tend the chickens at dawn, water them, collect the eggs, do a rough count to see if any pillage had taken place by man or beast, then feed the horses before the hands came to saddle them and ride off.

Sally would come down at dawn, draw and boil water, make coffee, prepare the food and the table.

Georgia brought the egg basket in and noticed Sally sitting in her chair. All the preparations for breakfast were done, but Sally rarely sat down until evening—ever.

"Sally? You feelin' all right? Why are you settin'? I don't mind. It's just not like you."

Georgia looked at the large, peaceful figure in the chair with her hands folded in her lap like Georgia had seen her do in church so many times. She watched closely to see if Sally's chest would rise and fall with breath. It did not.

She reached out to touch Sally's face with the back of her

fingers, as her palms were too rough to touch a delicate cheek. The touch landed on skin that had lost its glow and its warmth from within. Such a discovery can carry its profound message a great distance. All the men must have sensed something important and sacred had happened. Maybe it was just that Sally hadn't rung the bell, or called out, but they came into the house with their hats in their hands, silent and somber.

Georgia's plan to purge herself and seek Blue Stone couldn't be carried out this year. But the last conversation she had with Sally was etched into her memory and she reviewed it nearly every day.

Wade helped pack Sally's belongings and prepare for winter. He worked inside and outside beside Georgia, helping with her chores. Then she would help him outside with as many of his as she could. The other hands got used to the unusual pair and understood their unique bond.

No woman came to take Sally's place or to help Georgia with the farm. From October to January, letters were sent to Ruth McDaniels with no reply. Finally, late in January, Ruth showed up with two women and a wagonload of lumber.

"Well, look at you!" Ruth's arms sprung open and she reached out to hug Georgia then remembered how standoffish the girl could be and stopped her arms in mid-stretch.

"Mornin', ma'am. It's real good to see you again. We surely miss Sally a lot and have missed you, too."

"Did Sally's things get sent to the O'Connors in Chicago?"

"Yes, ma'am. Wade took them before the first snow."

Georgia went to the wagon to inspect the contents. "What's all this for, Missus? You having a baby and gonna build it a room?"

"My, no! Mister wants to build on to the house to make more room for all of us. Even though he is so rarely here, he is thinking of the time when he will be too tired to leave."

Georgia listened intently. "Where are these ladies going to live? There's no room inside. Oh, I guess they can share Sally's bed."

"Yes, I brought them to help you. They can do all the inside work and you can be outside, where you prefer to be, anyway."

"Yes, Missus, that would be good, but I ..."

"Come on, let's get them settled and out of this bitter cold. That's the problem with blue sky in the winter. No clouds to hold any warm in."

Ruth buzzed about the two newcomers, chatting about the bed space and where to put their things.

"Oh for heavens' sake." She said "I haven't even introduced you all."

The moment Georgia dreaded had arrived.

"Alberta, Ethel, this is Georgia. She has worked for us for a long time and knows every nook and cranny of this house and farm." The ladies looked at each other first, not knowing if they should try to shake her hand. They curtsied instead and Georgia mumbled, "How'd do."

Just to be courteous, she asked, "Are you sisters?"

The girls looked nothing alike, but it was a reasonable thing to ask anyway.

Alberta was tall and slender with almost flesh free fingers. She was wiry and Georgia thought the woman was most likely a lot stronger than she looked. She was right.

Ethel was only about five feet tall in her high-heeled shoes. Her hands were already very knarled with arthritis. Georgia wondered just what the Missus had in mind for this poor soul to be doing on this busy, expansive farm. She looked at the soft face and decided whatever Ethel couldn't do—Alberta would take up the slack. She was right.

Georgia didn't want to get to know the new women and kept to herself, except to show them the lay of the land as far as the inside was concerned. Sally had left a big empty space inside, and Georgia wasn't ready to fill it with the new girls.

She was determined to go as soon as these girls could do it all by themselves. When she was finally able to tell the Missus her plan, Ruth nodded her head in understanding, but her face became sad and her voice lost its sparkle.

The seemingly sudden wish for wanderlust happened because Georgia's thoughts had been reflecting on her last conversations with Wade and Sally.

Wade had remarked, "A life with no goals, direction or purpose is without meaning and open to soul-sucking influences." He had said those words before she left this farm the first time. Now he said them again, but only with his eyes, as she and he stood, wordless, hands touching, saying goodbye.

Her heart heard his message. This next ride, this next adventure, did have purpose. Before she would seek Blue Stone, she wanted to find out what it was that had guided her, protected her, and allowed, enabled or ignored the evil that inhabited the world.

People are the instrument for evil, she concluded. Blue Stone was probably not evil throughout. *Who could demonstrate overcoming human leanings toward evil?*

Julia. Sally. Ebony. Clara. Wade. They all had an abiding faith in something outside a human's ability to manipulate. This is what she sought.

Even though her destination was unknown, the *something* that had guided her in the past urged her on, straight ahead. Riding away from the McDaniels farm this time, there was purpose. She directed Moonshine to gallop with the speed and rhythm of a heartbeat, and as she rode she meditated.

She thought of Wade's words and her daydream took her to the day and time he said them. The near-musical clang of Wade working on a horseshoe had drawn her into the barn. He continued working, apparently not noticing her. A kitten hopped out of the hay. Georgia plopped down to play with it. She teased it with a piece of straw and delighted in the kitten's exuberant leaps of wide-eyed anticipation.

Perhaps it was this carefree moment, which sparked in him the thought that she had been wandering without purpose. Dozens of drifters had come through here for temporary work. They had no purpose except to survive. Some only wanted to survive till they could get drunk. All but one had claimed no family, no home, and none— except that one—had believed in anything, not even the spirits that he and Georgia believed in.

"What do you want your life to be about?" he blurted.

Georgia snapped her head up in astonishment. "What do you

mean?"

"Life—a person's life—must have some purpose, goal, or direction. Something to accomplish or leave behind that makes the world better."

A million things passed through her mind so quickly that she couldn't grasp any of them. She felt dizzy. "I ... I don't ...," she stammered, then her demeanor changed completely. "What is *your* purpose, your direction?" these were the first arrows she had ever directed at Wade. "Are you going to shovel manure, cut crops and stay here—the only one like you? Does that make you special? Give you purpose?" She stopped.

"My purpose is to be a person that defies other people's assumptions about me. My purpose is to become a better person tomorrow than I am today. My direction is *up*—aiming at what I believe God wants me to be. If He wants me to have a companion, I believe no power on earth can keep it from happening."

He waited for a response for a few breaths, and then he went on, "What do you believe in?"

She stood up quickly, the kitten scampered off.

Now was no time to speak without weighing her words or divorcing them from her heart. She realized, as she put them together before speaking, standing to face this challenge, exactly what she did believe in.

"You and Sally have showed me that a Creator takes care of those He has His own plans for. You and she convinced me that the Creator uses all that He created to help those plans. An elk led you to me, a hawk attacked the man who was attacking me, and your mother bore you here in a place safe enough to leave you so you could live. Sally believed that everything happens for a reason we may never know the purpose of it."

Wade stood amazed at what he was hearing. She continued.

"I believe if I have a purpose in His plan—like you—nothing on earth will keep it from happening. Something is urging me to go to the Sacred Mountains. I don't even know where they are, but I believe that force will guide me there."

Those conversations played in her mind while she galloped

toward a destiny she couldn't envision.

The throbbing of the hooves brought her back to the moment of her journey when her purpose was to seek undeniable guidance—not wait for it to come to her. The Sacred Mountains were a universe away.

But it was not meant to be. Another merciless, snowstorm drove her back. Mid-October often brought snow to this part of the world but nothing like this one. She barely made it to the farm, leading the horse because he couldn't manage the deep snow with her weight on his back.

Through eyelashes nearly sealed with snow and ice, she peered at a blurry form, moving as if in slow motion to catch her before she fell face first into a drift. Frank recalled how Wade had brought her to this farm after a blizzard those many years ago as he took the horse from her and settled it in the barn, while she struggled to her feet.

Sally had reassured her years before, "Those sacred mountains, wherever they are, will most certainly still be there in the spring. As mountains go, they don't move much."

Georgia was confused, disheartened and felt abandoned by the spirit that she expected to guide her. Nothing anyone did lifted her spirits.

Nineteen

Life Goes On for Georgia—1860

Georgia stayed four more years at the McDaniels farm, but when the family built the bigger house and hired three maids to take care of it, she left.

Every time a town got big enough to have a church, she left there, too.

Mountains abounded everywhere. She drifted from the Ozarks to Wyoming and down to New Mexico. None of them called to her. Her dreams were uneventful and didn't give much guidance, either. Eventually she even forgot to be looking for it and survival was again the focus, until the day a beautiful yellow butterfly gracefully alighted on her arm, she heard its simple message—"It's time"—as it rested on her arm and slowly waved its wings.

Timeliness had always been a strong indicator that guidance was in play. All the past months—or had it been years—she had drifted with no signal to go or to stay in any particular place. Now, here it was.

The creature stayed nearby and hung on a low leaf while she packed up camp and saddled her steed. The moment she mounted, the butterfly lifted off and drifted toward a mountain that stood out alone on the horizon. Georgia followed the best she could but lost sight of the guide in the glare of the sun. But, by now, she was certain, as she always was when mystical things happened, that the guide intended her to get to the mountain. She put all her energy into reaching it before sunset.

The sun, now obscured by the mountain, was bowing out. Georgia bedded down at the base of it and focused on plans for the morning. What to bring, what to leave behind?

At daybreak she packed up, washed a bit, and waited for

another sign.

"Come to the top." A voice compelled her to conquer this peak. It was commanding but loving. She obeyed.

Snakes had curled themselves up on a dozen or more rocks near the beginning of the trail to warm themselves in the hot morning air.

"Go forward, they will not harm you," the voice urged convincingly.

"Good horse, keep moving," Georgia said reassuringly. He plodded onward, nervously tossing his head and glancing back at her with near panic in his eyes.

Passing the snakes with no incident increased her confidence in the source that led her.

The base of the mountain was wide and its climb was easy at the beginning. Scrub and solid earth provided good footing for the horse's feet and the comfort of the ride.

Gradually, the landscape shifted to stonier ground and larger boulders all around. Thorn-covered scrub snuggled in huge clumps against the massive sheltering rocks, and marble-sized stones kept getting caught in the horse's shoes. After stopping a dozen times to remove the stones, she became convinced the horse would have to be set loose. She stopped to evaluate the possibilities for the best path. All visible paths ended in stones and boulders that no horse could manage.

"Pardner, head on back." The horse whinnied his objection as she removed his bridle and saddle. A canteen, a bed roll, and a bow were all she kept from the fully stocked saddle bags and leather bags hanging from the saddle horn. One sharp slap on the horse's haunch turned him away from her.

Her climb became a crawl on all fours and grit filled the spaces of her teeth, nails, and all bodily creases. Sweat made a glue that held the grit in place and turned it to a cement-like substance. The silt was the home for a variety of ants that made their way down her sleeves and up her pant legs. Such annoyances multiplied and began to wear away at her resolve to follow through.

"Whose idea was this, anyway? This is pointless. There is nothing at the top of this mountain that will teach me anything I don't know already." Climbing in such steep terrain made it impossible to look around and scope out the surroundings for a better path to avoid obstacles and threats.

Clawing into the dirt, and grasping the rock above or beside her while keeping her footing and balance, narrowed her vision to what was right in front of her nose. But she kept on reaching above, digging in her toes, and pushing her torso up and over boulder after boulder, dirt falling in her eyes and ants crawling in her ears, because she knew the voice she had heard believed so strongly in her. She had to return such confidence with all her heart. In her deepest self, she understood that 'The Voice' knew her perseverance would make her successful.

As she climbed higher the sun's light was deceivingly bright. Shadows filled the landscape below but kept her mountain lit until she reached the flattened top. Stars were popping out as the sun bowed out of sight, leaving nothing but remembrance of its light.

She built a small fire and looked for anything that could be used for survival. The voice was silent. Only her own thoughts rambled through her mind. She spoke aloud for the company of her words.

"Well, here I am. I don't see anything out of the ordinary here. My horse is somewhere unfamiliar to him, and I have no real reason to be here, except that a formless, nameless force compelled and commanded me to come. Now what?"

She waited. No response. Only the murmurings of the fire, with snaps for emphasis now and then, entered her ears.

No fire could be made warm enough at this elevation unless she built it big enough to be a danger to the foliage that had layered this mound for centuries. She resolved to sleep under the blanket she had expected to use as ground cover and snuggled as close as possible to the waning fire.

In spite of the grit grinding its way into her skin, the effort of the day put her in a deep sleep right away. Her consciousness was available to watch and listen without rational thought interrupting or misinterpreting. The dream began.

Suddenly she rose up and flew through the roof of a house, flying through the night air faster than she had ever moved before. There was no wind resistance and no sound as she flew. The land below was filled with creatures, but none took notice—until there was a lake and a large wolf, staring at the sky.

Her consciousness landed softly beside it. His golden eyes held wisdom she was unable to fathom.

He spoke to her. "Your faith has brought you here."

Then the wolf said, "Stretch out your hand and touch my cheek."

She did.

A power greater than anything she had ever seen or felt surged up through her arm. A light with a glow she had never seen before emitted from her arm and hand. Without pain, her arm felt like jelly, and she had to hold it with her other hand. When she did so, she brought it to her chest. Her heart beat strong and clear through the jelly-like hand and she felt her whole being throb with its power.

Light formed before her. The light filled with colors and became a kaleidoscope changing from deep purple, to red, then blue, then yellow, then green. Green formed itself into leaves and grasses, and she felt her bare feet standing on it.

A being made of light moved closer, the voice that compelled her to climb the mountain, said, "Welcome."

Behind and next to the being of light were Julia and Sean and Phineas and Franklin, all smiling at her proudly.

The being of light spoke again. "You have always had one question on your heart. You can ask it now."

"You know my question. Must I say it?"

All the spirits present waited patiently and she could feel their love and hear their loving thoughts.

Sally forgave her for staying away. Franklin poured out gratitude to her for caring for Ebony. Julia and Phineas beamed with pride for her spiritual growth. Sean was a grown man and proud of his sister for the same reason. Accepting this outpouring of love was hard for her and she curled into a ball weeping.

When the emotional flood was over she sat on her heels and asked, "Did Blue Stone really love my mother?" The response was immediate.

"Find your father." Words that took her breath away. "Learn for yourself his true character and ask him your question if you will still need to know." A truth she had always known, but fear had stopped her many times. Wave after wave of grief surged within to release her shame.

Nothing more could be done to assure her that guidance had accompanied her for her entire life helping when necessary, holding back when she needed to grow on her own.

In the first light of dawn she squelched the fire, packed up her bed roll, filled her lungs with the cool, clear air and headed down the mountain.

With every step down she was filled with gratitude and peace, like the climb had held anticipation. Saddle and bridle were still in the brush where she hid them and the horse was waiting near a stand of trees at the bottom of the hill, chomping on grass.

Writing in her journals took on new meaning, and she continued sending them on to Clara and Ebony.

The search for her father didn't happen right away. Settling somewhere safe to absorb the new understanding and all the meanings of the spiritual gifts was her priority.

Time slipped away.

Charting the days gave way to losing track of the years.

More of her hair lost it's black with red highlights giving way to more gray, but the distinctive lock next to her face still stood out clearly.

Calluses, knots and a variety of scars turned her hands into a sculptor's dream—or nightmare—depending on the skill level of the artist.

All of her limbs had reminders of physical collisions on her life's path. Her legs had long ragged stripes from falling or being thrown onto barbed wire fences. Her arms bore symbolic tattoos from scrapes with rocks, branches, and critters she had tangled with—wild and domestic, man and animal.

Life's lessons polished the rough edges from her heart, and as a result, she learned the value and rewards of forgiveness.

Wade had demonstrated that shedding resentments, leaves room for understanding the nature of ignorance and how to release one's own hate and reject the hate of others.

Now she too, had a strong faith in a guide that gave love to all. Circumstances had shown her how reliable that source can be.

Years of life, dreams, death, birth nourished her, ripened her, changed her, made her ready.

Now the most difficult lesson of all. Patience.

Twenty

Georgia and Webster Meet – She is Forty-five Years Old

Journal note: 1878 –*"April is a busy month for farmers and ranchers. The stock is reproducing and the ground is still being plowed and planted. All the house repairs and deep cleaning chores, put off in winter and pointless during the snowmelts, are started in March, if possible, and continue through April. The Gardener family won't be back until May when all the hardest work is done."*

Georgia wrote that she had helped the neighbors gather cowboys to get the branding done. She helped the women with their house chores and mended a few roofs, pens and fences to give the men time to find and collect all the animals. Every night, well past sundown, she was still doing catch-up chores, cleaning pots, sharpening kitchen tools, peeling potatoes, caring for sickly calves or colts, and dragging her aching, forty-five-year-old bones to a lumpy bed in a drafty room.

She loved dawn, especially in April. The men 'geed and hawed' to the tune of the jingling rigging and harnesses. The earth exhaled from the plows opening the packed dirt, and the aroma of rich soil inspired earthy thoughts and urges in all directions. A few hours later she could hear the bees humming over at the hollow tree, their wispy legs laden with pollen from the apple and plum blossoms dressing up the trees. She barely had time to notice, but these sensory delights were not lost to her. She took mental pictures and absorbed the colors and smells and saved them in a secret place inside.

The day before, the ranch hands down the road had found a dozen dead lambs, and accusations were made that the cow men on this ranch had poisoned the ewes and caused them to abort. Resolving such disputes had to wait because work took precedence.

Georgia never took sides and had worked both sheep and

cattle ranches with no preference. She also never took part in the tongue-lashings when the hands egged each other on. Today there had been a lot of tension in the air, and the men's work was not getting done. Even though she was not the foreman of this ranch, she felt the responsibility for keeping it running smoothly.

At the end of this particularly long and difficult day, her attention was on the moon. It was close to full, and as it rose, she held up a saucer at arms' length to compare the size. It took the whole saucer to cover the face of the moon. Only minutes after laying down her head, she was in a deep sleep.

The dream that started was one she had been having for months.

It began where her day left off, by measuring the night sphere, just as she had before her eyes closed. Still dreaming, she put the saucer down, and the nearly full moon stared back at her with its startled expression. The hill, twelve miles away, provided the moon its slow, dramatic entrance and was the stage for an approaching horse and rider. Their silhouette stood out against the face of the glowing globe like a shadow play in motion.

Horse and rider charged onward with determination but not speed, with purpose but not aggression, never wavering, coming straight for her. The rider didn't follow the gentle switchbacks of the path that the wagon used. They made their own shortcut—a quicker, more direct route.

"What a magnificent horseman. How—confidently he rides— at night—over unfamiliar, untrodden ground." Her dream self stood transfixed, casting a spell by wishing with her whole being to draw him nearer.

When the horseman reached her side, he reached down and pulled her up onto the horse, and they rode together full speed into the night.

She didn't drift slowly from the depths of her dream world. She woke instantly, with her heart racing and a strong sense that the dream was a foretelling.

The morning was a gray, overcast spring day. The flowers next to the farmhouse were all closed up and misted with condensed fog.

After a dream like that, she expected a bright day with birds chirping in mixed chorus.

However, the only bird sounds were monotonous Mourning Doves, who instinctively showed up and added their mood-altering coos to foggy, overcast mornings. The dreariness stole the magical anticipation the dream had given her and clouded her memory of it.

Georgia pumped water with listless effort. Then, with a mechanical stare, she fed the animals. Her hair sat on the back of her head in a twisted bundle with strands of hair dangling down. They looked a lot like the tail feathers of the hens she was feeding. The chickens puttered and muttered around her feet in the yard. As her mother used to do, she answered in perfect imitation of their conversational clucks and drawls.

After collecting all the fresh eggs, she cooked them for the hands. The men strode in, one at a time. The daily routine was to come in, take a biscuit from under a cloth on the stove. She'd hand them a plate and utensils, then that man would pour his own coffee and sit, the next one would come in, and the ritual would repeat until the table that held eight was full. Then she'd put the eggs and gravy on their plates.

There was an empty seat at the table.

"Where's Jake the Snake?" Georgia asked.

"Took out early, said he heard somethin' out by the corral," one of the men said.

"How could he hear anything over there? I can't hear you boys, when you're making a ruckus, when I'm here in the house," Georgia mused.

"He's always had an ear like that," one fella said. "I wouldn't discount it, ma'am. Part Indian, I think. 'Course, he couldn't claim it."

"Seen him chase down rabbits on foot. Catch a critter by the ears and let it go. Does it just for fun," a second man added.

"Seen him do it a coupla times," another chimed in.

"Yup, Injun. Gotta be," another remarked.

The men ate and drank in relative silence until Jake was heard outside in conversation with another man.

"Hey, boys, meet my new pal, Webster." Jake announced

cheerfully as he entered the kitchen.

Multiple "howdy doo's" and grunts of recognition went around the table as Webster removed his hat and nodded to each man.

His sight landed on Georgia, just as hers froze on him. The light from the grayish morning glared behind him from the doorway, and all she could see clearly was his outline. The outline matched the size and shape of the man in her dream. She gave it no thought, but the immediate attraction to him made her find an excuse to leave the room.

"I'll get you a chair, Mr. Webster," she said as she spun on the ball of her foot and disappeared through the door.

"Don't bother, George. He can have my spot," Charlie offered. He shot straight up, swung his leg up, over and behind the chair, and stood behind it in a single move.

"George? Did you just call that lady George?" Webster sounded appalled.

"Her name is Georgia, but we've always called her George. Happened some time ago, some farmhand called her that cuz he didn't know she was a woman. She only recently started wearing a dress 'cuz she works round the house and yard now. 'Sides, she said it's alright to call her George. Really." Webster shook his head. "I don't think I'll be able to call her George, or even Georgia. What's her last name?"

Every man's face went blank, motions froze in place with forks or cups in mid-air and mouths open.

A.J. spoke first. "Welllllllll, I don't rightly recall anyone ever sayin' it."

The men unfroze.

Georgia returned with a three-legged milking stool. It was obvious to everyone but her that it was much too short for the table. The men grinned at each other. They knew why her mind was addled.

"Sorry, mister, this is all I could find on short notice."

She had taken off the apron, with its smears of batters and sauces and splotches of lard, coffee and other unknown substances. The tail feathers of her hair were now neatly tucked up into the knot at the nape of her neck, and other strays had been flattened and tacked down with her saliva. The finishing touch of a bonnet covered the rest of her untended hair.

Looking up, she noticed Webster was already sitting behind an empty plate and she put down the stool.

"Say, George, this fella wants to know what your last name is. I dunno why he'd wanna know secha thing, but he asked us, and—I'll be hanged—we found out nobody knows."

"That's because I don't want you no-accounts to know it. If I ever do tell ya', it'll be on my deathbed so's you'll know what name to put on my tombstone." Her retort feigned irritation, but her glance was serious enough to signal the regulars to leave.

They did, en masse. The house vibrated with chairs scooting and boots stomping from the men racing each other to get out the door.

"Now, then, what was your name again, mister?" With deliberate effort to please, she picked out the two best biscuits and the most perfect eggs and gently and gracefully set the plate in front of Webster, as though he were a prince.

She returned to the stove with his cup to fill it with hot coffee.

"Webster," he replied and continued, "The young Indian fella I was talking to earlier said the owners of this ranch are away. Said you're in charge around here."

"The Gardener family owns it. They have relatives in Texas they are staying with until mid-May"

"Ma'am, you might think I'm crazier than a horse on locoweed, but … I feel like I know you. Do you …? Er … I mean … can that be true?"

"It happens … sometimes … when we meet … a stranger." She heard herself reply shyly. She couldn't believe herself. She was never coy. But the magnetism crushing its way through her chest had to be moderated somehow. This feeling terrified and fascinated her at the same time. She waited for him to speak next while she took a deep breath and reined in the horses rearing and charging inside her rib cage.

"I asked the men for your last name so I could address you

properly." The words didn't fit the scruffy man before her, with threadbare cuffs, long johns peeking through gaping holes in the elbows, and trousers that quite obviously only got washed in a stream.

She smiled at the incongruous remark. "The only men who know that are dead." Since it was true, her serious expression and the tone in her voice belied her playful intent.

Clank! Webster dropped his fork. The sound punctuated his surprise. His bug-eyed expression was her payoff.

They laughed together and each heard the music their patterns and tones produced. First harmonizing, then matching perfectly in intensity and pitch. Like two twitterpated birds, chirping and twirling closely together, birds in ecstasy at finding the perfect partner. Then they stopped—in perfect unison. It was too much for both of them; nonetheless, both knew something major had happened.

A door—that she alone entered—opened to him, and she softly replied, "It's Dunbar. My full name is Savannah Georgia Dunbar." He couldn't know the full meaning of this moment.

"Well, Miss … is it Miss? Dunbar?" his words were hushed and hopeful. He could sense he was about to tread in a place few had been.

"Georgia. Please, you must call me Georgia." It had been decades since she had gone by Savannah Dunbar, an aspect of herself that she had kept in that secret room, first out of self-preservation, then out of habit. The door to her soul was wide open now. She stood in the middle of it with anticipation.

"Georgia, if, in fact, I don't know you as I feel like I do, I believe it's of vital importance that I *do* get to know you. My life's guided by everything that happens to me, and everyone I meet has meaning. I have put my life in the hands of the Creator and try to listen to Him when He directs me."

"I probably look like your favorite aunt, or some other woman who has been kind to you in your life. That's why you think you know me." Her voice rose a little with each sentence. No matter what her words were saying, her heart was pounding; the wild horses raring inside would not be quieted.

She longed for him to see through the space in the door she had nearly—but not quite—closed. But she needed time, time to get used to the things Webster was making her feel. Webster had swept in too far, too quickly, had made himself too much at home without giving her time to adjust to his presence. She felt dizzy. He made her afraid of her feelings and she began to close the door to her heart in self-preservation.

She stiffened her spine and went on. "You a preacher?" Before he could answer she added, "If you are, I have to tell you right off ... I got my own way of thinking. God doesn't live in little wooden buildings. He's everywhere—but mostly out there, in the wind, water, sky, earth, creatures and everything alive. He's not stuck in a box and visited once a week by people who don't live by His words, anyway."

Why did I say that? How could I tell him so much? What is happening here?

Webster stood at that door, expecting to have it slammed in his face but willing to block it open and step in, anyway. Something he never would have done before.

She wasn't finished. "Maybe you have seen me in some town or another in passing, but I'm certain you don't know me and I have no such notions as you about being guided or protected by a God!"

The lie was meant to protect her heart that was wildly out of control this moment. She more than shared his beliefs; she was, at this point in her life, living them.

Webster understood he'd come too close and stepped back a pace or two, but his belief was strong. He'd been brought here—to meet her, perhaps to hold her and make her his wife. For him, God's wishes were the most important to heed. Her rejection of God and his concept of God didn't erase or negate His existence or change Webster's faith a hair's breadth.

He understood people who felt as she did. They'd generally had much suffering in their life, usually as children. He also believed he was the answer to her pain. His way of thinking was that what she needed most was to experience happiness in her life, "I have no wish to frighten or anger you. Your hospitality and generosity speak clearly

132

about the kindness of your character. Please accept my apology for my forthrightness."

Oh no. Perfect. She thought. *Just perfect.*

His words were out of character with the rugged drifter that uttered them. She reviewed her rude response, regretting it immediately.

"Mr. Webster …"

"Webster is my first name, Michaels is my last name. Initials W.M. The same upside down and backwards—makes a perfect brand." The mood lightened as he had intended.

Georgia added, "But, as a brand, it's much too easy to forge." She pulled out a hairpin and bent it to match his description.

They laughed again and the music they made was just like the first time. That door to her heart reopened wider. She wasn't sure if she had done it or if it was an invisible force beyond her control. It didn't matter. He reached through it and led her out.

Georgia really looked at him now—taking in his smile and the shades of blue in his eyes. She could tell the wrinkles at the edges of his eyes were from squinting in bright sun and from smiling. His brow was nearly smooth, with only a faint hint of a line under the tan line from his hat. The age carved into his face was appealing.

She tilted her head and studied the rest of his face, his hair, the way he held himself—straight and tall—regal-like, but not stiff or stuffy—and then—the hands. Georgia always noted a man's hands and was of a mind that very few men's hands could be called graceful or smooth without being foppish and small.

These hands were held confidently, with a manly grace. The fingers were calloused on the inside but outwardly as smooth as a marble statue she had seen once. An indescribable quality in those hands, like those of the statue, drew her attention and held it. She fell instantly in love with those hands. A strong breeze swept past that inner doorway, breathing a promise of a new chapter for her life.

"Tell me more about your thoughts of being guided. How did you come to believe that way?" It had been too much of a wonderful coincidence to think that this man thought the same way she did. Her initial reaction was an old reaction to his unexpected response. Her apology was implied by the tone of her voice.

"Well, Miss Georgia," he began, "that can be long in the telling, and I reckon those hard-workin' ranch hands wouldn't much abide me eating this food and not putting in some time out there with them. Can you use my help for just room and board?"

"Of course, Mr. Michaels."

He added, "Then would you honor me by calling me Webster and accompanying me this evenin' and talkin'—away from the others? You can show me your favorite sights on this ranch, or we can stay inside by the fire." His voice was filled with hopefulness.

"I love...I much prefer being outside," she said, "especially in the evening. I'll arrange it. Now, when you find the men, you should ask A.J. what he wants you to do out there. He's the tallest, skinniest fella. Wears a gray hat with a leather band—it has silverwork on it."

Webster took his plate to the wash tub then gathered his cup and utensils. Georgia swept the crumbs away and pushed in the chair. It was as if they were doing a well-rehearsed dance as they sashayed around the room. Their movements had the same rhythm; there was no awkwardness and there was a 'knowing' of what the other was going to do next.

Webster tipped his hat as he stepped out on the porch. Sunlight emphasized the contrast between his dark skin and the whiteness of his teeth when he grinned broadly enough to show dimples, lots of dimples, those horses inside Georgia were chomping at the bit.

Georgia waved as she said, "Be ready for razzing and horseplay from the boys. Always check both stirrups before you mount—probably a fresh cow patty in one or the other. Check your rope, too, might be a garter snake wrapped up in it. I don't think these boys ever did grow up.

Twenty-One

Weeding the Garden

She ignored other chores and headed for the garden. Digging in the dirt, exposing roots of voracious weeds and freeing up space for new growth, was in tune with her thoughts and burned off some of the energy—or whatever it was—making her hands shake and knees weak. Plunging the shovel deep into the earth and helping it breathe; she replayed what he had said about being under God's care.

Ebony Rose had introduced her to the idea that God was truly in charge of everything and even the horrible things that happened to people could be seen as a benefit to a person. For most of her life, Georgia had refused to embrace such thoughts. There didn't seem to be any sign of this benevolent caretaker in her life. In the first place, she still presumed that some wild-eyed Indian—resulting in Georgia's own existence—had impregnated her mother against her will. Then, the man who married her mother, knowing her condition, was killed when his horse tripped and trapped the man beneath him. If that wasn't enough, her mother and brother were both dead by the time Georgia was sixteen.

From the time she was attacked, she wrestled with the anger she felt toward God, and took it out on most of the men she met. Every death that took people she cared about awakened rage and anger and her lack of control, then took her into a deep and long-lasting depression. The visit to the mountaintop had purged most of that bitterness. Whatever was left was up to her to deal with. She no longer spat out her anger toward men, but she didn't let any of them in through that secret door Webster had just gracefully waltzed through, either.

Here was a man—one of those untrustworthy creatures—who touted a deep, abiding belief in a God who guides one's life. She was powerfully drawn to this man before knowing anything about his ideas.

Each weed she pulled from the garden opened another space within, making room for another's thoughts and opinions. Extending the rows and adding seeds, she was preparing soil for another being to occupy, share and grow with her in life. She wanted this change. She made room for it. The light he brought into her life overcame her fear of the unknown.

The end of the day was a contradiction to the beginning. Hopeful, fresh colors filled the sky in late afternoon. That led to a sunset with one long, full cloud over the sun, which dispersed its rays of light. Those fingers reached for and touched the edge of the horizon beyond the ranch. Georgia looked at her own fingers during these moments of meditation. She was satisfied that they had been useful for all these years, and waves of gratitude flowed from her heart toward those fingers of light. She was standing behind the hen house, absorbed in this beauty, when a voice—not her own—joined her thoughts.

"God is painting the skies and sending His love to you."

Webster was bending low over her shoulder, speaking directly in her ear, like the unseen whisperers that guided her alone on the prairie. His words found another place to rest. Her heart was opened, pouring out her gratitude for the beauty; those tender words planted themselves deep in the center of it.

This rugged drifter had captured her affection when he first sat at the table. Now, those few words completed a bond that was new and full of mysteries to be explored and unwrapped. They both had a lifetime of stories to tell and pains to heal and life lessons already lived to share. A tumbleweed existence full of adventure had been the way of life for each of them. Finding each other—at this point in their lives—was completely unexpected.

"Why do you think I stopped here at this ranch?" Webster began.

"I supposed it was because you could smell the food cooking and you were hungry."

"I have food in my saddlebags. Enough to get me to a town and buy more or find a place to eat there. And I can hunt, if I choose."

"Why *did* you stop here, then?"

"Can you open your head to take in a new idea?"

He couldn't know she had been preparing for it all day. "Go ahead," she said, "I think I can take in whatever you have to say."

"Last night I had a dream ..."

For the first time that day, she recalled her own dream, and the realization it had been foretelling sent a burst of electricity through her body. She caught her breath and her eyes widened as she blurted, "You! It was you!"

Webster could see in her eyes that they had had the same dream. He continued. "Yes. I was riding—nearly galloping—the moon was at my back and I could clearly see ahead of me "

"But all I could see was your shape against the moon." she added.

"I was urged to keep going forward and I didn't know why or where, but I had to obey the urging" he said.

"So confident and brave in the night, through untouched ground, like you knew every stone, gopher hole and..." she said as she moved closer to him.

"Then I saw this ranch house—and you, your face—with a look of expectation. You were waiting—for me. You dreamed of me last night, didn't you?" he finished her thought.

"I couldn't see your face. I could only feel the strength of your purpose to get here, to find me. And I wished you to come to me, to help you find me. But it is so late in my life, I don't understand why now? Do you?"

"I don't ask why when it comes to what God gives me in life—good, bad, indifferent, boring, funny, or heartbreaking, and I've had plenty of all of those things. I don't ask why. Never have. I just accept what He gives me and try to be grateful for all of it."

She couldn't believe her ears or her eyes.

He went on. "You, you are a gift I could never have imagined for myself. Whatever time He has allowed us to share—even if it's just right now this night, this moment—it's perfect. I'll treasure it forever, and if I were to live forever, I wouldn't be able to express the full measure of my thankfulness."

Her face glistened with trails of tears in the fading light, Georgia reached up to touch his face and opened her mouth to speak, but he spoke first, "We don't need words now, " he said brushing her lips like a feather with his magnificent fingers.

"Shhhh," she whispered. Her breath made a bridge between them.

Soul to soul they exchanged thoughts and feelings. Those souls shared a union which lives in eternity—fully clothed, yet completely exposed to each other—without speaking. For a moment they transcended time. That moment would live in infinity, to be visited at will for the rest of their existence. For the first time in her life, Georgia understood how her mother loved the Indian.

When the moment melted back into this reality, they talked about a future together and walked the horses into the barn.

"Are you obligated to stay here or can you leave any time you choose?" Webster asked.

"I'm allowed to leave any time, but to be fair to the owners and the men, I should make arrangements for someone to take my place. The Gardeners should be back soon. They left for the winter and I got a letter a few weeks ago that they're on their way home, but there have been travel delays, and there may be more. They want to be here by mid-May."

"You must come with me to meet Blue Stone, an important Indian leader. I expect to find him in June near the Sun Dance site. This is such an honor, because the place is kept secret and few whites have ever been allowed to see it."

She withdrew in revulsion at 'Blue Stone,' even from Webster's fine lips. She took off her bonnet so quickly that the strings snapped like a whip.

"What's wrong? What ... did I ...? You are part Indian, aren't you? I mean, your skin and ..." He stopped abruptly. For the first time in the hours they had spent together, he noticed the pronounced white streak in her graying hair. Georgia had put several steps of distance between them and was looking at him—for the first time—like he was a stranger.

"Your hair! You're Blue Stone's daughter. You are, aren't

you?"

No response.

For the first time since being on the mountain, she had to face the fact that she had not looked for him. The guilt of not seeking him had built up resentment and self-anger and she aimed it at Blue Stone out of habit. Her deepest pool of hatred was still saved for him and she couldn't face him out of revulsion.

"Have you met him? Do you know him?"

The words burst out of her. "I know only that he made me against my mother's will. That he's probably going around raping as many women as he can get his hands on. That he's probably so filled with hate and whiskey he can't tell you his own name. That he's the coldest, most selfish thing on two legs, and if I ever do meet him, I'll scalp him myself and send him shamed into the Great Beyond! Isn't that how it works?"

Webster let it all lay on the barn floor with the excrement of the horses and mildewed hay. Based on the moment they had just shared, he knew this was not what was in her heart. He gave her time to hear her own words before he said, "You've never met him or anyone that knows him!"

"I made a promise that I'd find him, but that was a long time ago and now I don't really care to."

Webster wasn't sure how much to tell her about his own promise to Blue Stone. "I promised..." he started to say then stopped, deciding now was not the moment. Instead he just added, "I'm going to the Sun Dance in June. He will be there and I want you with me. That's all I'm going to say."

He knew that telling his connection to Blue Stone now could kill any chance of bringing them together in peaceful conditions, and nothing more was said about it then.

Her sleep was uneasy that night, because of her hateful words aimed at Blue Stone echoing in her head throughout the long, dark hours.

After a few weeks of evening talks and fireside musings, never mentioning the Sun Dance again, their desire to create a life together began to shape the subject of their conversations. They talked about all of their major likes and dislikes. He described his 'dream house' that he had seen in New Mexico. She hadn't found hers, yet, but wanted to see his.

"Tell me about the house. Your house." She closed her eyes as he spoke in order to see with her mind's eye.

"There is something about that adobe house. The hands that made it worked their very sweat into every brick. A piece of their presence stays, infused into those bricks, the rooms, the air. This one—the one I will own someday—faces east for the sunlight to come in at dawn. We can add on to the house by making more bricks ourselves."

"I think I have been to New Mexico," she added, "but maybe it was only a dream. We could go there this winter or in the spring."

One night by the fire they both realized they kept using the pronoun 'we.' It was already decided, but unwritten, they were a 'we'. In another wordless moment he asked and she replied. And in that moment she embraced his concept that God had brought them together and would guide their lives, as He always had.

Mid-May found them busily arranging for a life together. The Gardeners paid the hands and chose a handful to keep on. The others had planned to move on, anyway, and Georgia and Webster made marriage plans. She stayed in the ranch house and he stayed in the bunkhouse, but they planned a life together.

Webster spoke matter-of-factly; she wouldn't respond to anything less. "I want to take you to meet a small band of Sioux so you can get to know them before we go to the Sun Dance. Are you ready to meet these people without hatred? That something in you that is akin to them needs to meet them and become acquainted with that."

By now she was willing to go any place on earth with or for him. Their talks had taught her his wisdom, gentleness, and purity of intentions. He had schooled her in the manners and customs of the Sioux culture. She was completely unaware the Sioux or any Indians had such refinements.

Her view of Indians changed with the knowledge Webster shared. The knot in her stomach no longer occurred at the mention of the word 'Indian', and she wanted to hear his stories about being with them and learning about them. When she heard they were guided by dreams and visions created by physical hardship, she understood how deep her connection with them ran.

She fully embraced the new philosophy when, Webster shared Blue Stone's words. "All the people are connected by the ever-present sound of the drum; the sound first heard in Mother's womb is the beating of her heart. It is the sound that every human heart makes with the first drum beat of life; in the drum the rumbling sound of thunder is captured and made to speak. This is the power of the drum." He didn't reveal the source.

That same cloudless day, thunder rumbled in the distance, Webster hopped onto Rambler, grabbed Georgia, and before she could ask what the heck was happening, he spurred the horse to a full gallop. She held onto her hat for dear life and her apron slapped against her exposed calves.

Her experiences with that kind of thunder were connected to flash floods, but this day she and Webster were many miles from any stream or river that could pose a threat. It wasn't long until they came upon a huge swath of freshly upturned and churned soil. There was a mixture of manure and urine odor with the rich earth.

Buffalo! She had never seen so many in one place.

They followed a path as wide as the Mississippi, until whooping could be heard.

Indians!

"Remember your manners. Your *Indian* manners." Webster shouted over his shoulder and blundered into the middle of the thundering herd of buffalo, the Indians and their horses throwing dirt clods. Buffalo came crashing to the ground and a dozen brown men would slide off their horses and guarantee a kill. Between thirty and fifty braves worked this herd; they killed—only taking what they needed—before stopping to butcher the carcasses into manageable pieces to carry back to the village on several travois.

The braves thought it was funny that Webster had brought his woman with him into the hunt and teased him about his 'shadow'. They threatened to name him "His Shadow Is a Woman." His easy-going manner helped him sail through the teasing and the feigned threats with a smile.

Georgia picked up on the mood but stayed in the background until they rode into the camp.

Women gave a joyous greeting to their successful hunters. The women's dresses, the teepees, and many tools and jewelry were laden with artful beadwork or painting. Everything she saw rang familiar within a primeval part of her.

Webster dismounted and led Rambler through the camp, while Georgia rode with queenly demeanor. They reached a large teepee with several horses behind it, and Webster eased Georgia down. He took tack and saddle off Rambler and urged him to the other horses.

Webster and Georgia stood outside the teepee, hand in hand.

She leaned to his ear and asked, "Is Blue Stone here?"

He gave a quick headshake, and then a woman emerged from the teepee.

"I greet my grandfather with open hand," Webster said, "I ask his permission to speak with him and present my woman."

They waited. Standing outside in the sun made sweat squiggle around under Georgia's hat.

The woman came out again and said that Medicine Bear asked them to come inside.

Once inside the teepee, Georgia removed her hat. The look of astonishment on the faces before her puzzled her at first. An ancient Indian, his middle-aged companion, and a young man stretched out on the fur hides all looked at her as though she had just completely disrobed. She quickly put her hat back on.

Medicine Bear's stunned expression was the most noticeable. He held his breath for a moment, then leaned toward Webster with a question in his eyes. Webster smiled and nodded at him. The woman saw that exchange and said something to the boy. He stood up as though his limbs were heavy branches and she made a short, terse comment to him and he hurried away from the teepee.

Rules of etiquette and custom make it rude to point out anyone's flaws or unique qualities. No one said a word about the outstanding streak in Georgia's hair. The men smoked and traded and spoke in their native tongue and in Indian sign language.

Webster confirmed the location of the Sun Dance that was to take place in June and then listened to the elder.

Georgia admired the beadwork on all the items in the teepee by pointing at them and smiling. The woman smiled back. Georgia pointed at her and then a piece of jewelry or art, and each time the woman would confirm whether it was her work or not by nodding or shaking her head.

When Webster was finished talking to the old man and his companion, he helped the old man to his feet and the men clasped hands. She noticed it wasn't in the white man's way. It looked like they might arm wrestle because their wrists were intertwined and the grasp went all the way up to the elbow. It was more expressive, intimate, and a stronger bond than a white man's handshake.

The men had sealed a trade or deal, and Webster went to his saddlebags and gave a finely crafted leather bag to the old man. The visitors were asked to wait for the boy to return before they departed.

Comfortable silence enveloped them as they stood together. Georgia took an elbow of Medicine Bear and the woman took the other. Just when Georgia could feel their silent thoughts completely harmonize, the boy came running back with a bundle under one arm. He stopped short next to Webster and handed it to him, grinning ear to ear, with rivulets of sweat running down his face that was beaming with smiles.

Whatever the youth had handed him was wrapped in a fox winter pelt. Webster knew bundles were usually wrapped with the fur on the inside, but the beauty of this extra-special fur deserved to be seen at first glance. He handed it to Georgia. It was very heavy, fifty pounds she guessed, as the weight of it lurched her body toward the ground before she had a good grasp on it.

"Wait until we get home," Webster growled. He had never sounded so stern.

The ride took longer going back, partly because most of it was uphill. Curiosity burned through her mind and a growing impatience and the heavy weight on her lap caused her ask several times, "Are you purposely going slower?"

He just grinned and urged Rambler to lope a little faster.

Twenty-Two

Nothing Is As Constant As Change

Firelight danced on every wall of the ranch house. Georgia sat in the rocker next to the fire, looking up at Webster standing beside her. She loved the way the fire enhanced his face. His eyes glowed from it, as he handed her the bundle. She opened it and stared in awe.

A doeskin dress, beaded and fringed, lay in her lap.

"This could be my wedding dress." Stroking it tenderly, the dress was soft as a cloud and felt like it was melting at the touch of her fingertips.

"If that is what you want. Are you sure that's what you want? I mean, the way you feel about 'Indians'..." he teased.

"You know they captured my heart. How could I help it? Everything felt like ... like ...home—the smells, the sounds, their clothes. And this ... marvelous, priceless gift. Why? Why would they do that?"

"I did a little trade for it, but it was the old woman's idea, when she heard we were to be married."

Georgia held the dress up next to her, checking for length. It was perfect. She held it out away from her to look at it from top to bottom while Webster explained the patterns in the beadwork.

On the front were two multi-colored, large butterflies and many other designs. "The butterfly signifies everlasting life. These have another symbol surrounding them. This round symbol with curved arms inside represents the ages of life. So these together are a blessing for a long life on earth and everlasting life in the same pattern."

At last, knowledge of the ancient culture whose influence was carved into her innermost being. Georgia was rapt.

He went on. "See how these broad lines connect the two

butterflies with a great shield in the center? When it's on you, it will look like a necklace, one whose chain can never be broken." His voice began to crack a little. "The shield contains several separate symbols that include sun rays. They mean constancy and that separate sun symbol means 'happiness'. The other decorations of rainbow-layered beading are creations of the artist with no particular meaning, other than the beauty they add."

Georgia was combing the long fringes that hung from the arms down to the bottom of the dress. The arm holes could accommodate a large arm, making room for growth and inner layers needed in cold weather. On each sleeve was a band of alternating colors that went down most of its length.

How many hours of work is this? How much patience and striving for perfection?

Webster watched her become absorbed in the intricate beading, and then he said, "Medicine Bear's niece was to be married during the Sun Dance, but she died last month. Her mother had been working on that dress from the day she was born. The young bride added the few lines of beadwork on the bottom, at the sleeve edges and there, at the neck opening.

"My God, this is even more precious than I imagined. You must take it back to them. It's too sentimental and valuable to their family. I have no right ... to ..."

Burning tears born of shame carved paths down her cheeks from eyes that felt like melting lumps of ice.

"Georgia, let God take it away. You don't need it anymore and there was no truth in it. It was all ignorant, spiteful lies. I can't take the dress back for many reasons, but most of all because of the spirit with which it was given. It was pure love and generosity. You don't throw back a gift like that." He held her as she released bitter tears.

The time was right, he thought. "Now, I'm going to tell you more about Blue Stone. The kind of man he is. The old man we visited is his uncle, Medicine Bear. Blue Stone is known for three things: He hunts only with the bow, because, as a young man, his medicine told him a rifle was an unfair disadvantage to the animal. He owned the largest piece of turquoise ever found. No one knows how he got it,

146

and it mysteriously disappeared after a Sun Dance. There is a fascinating legend about it.

"And lastly, at the same Sun Dance, he must have had a powerful spiritual experience, because on that day, his hair turned completely white.

Other than that, I can tell you what I've heard in the places I have been—trading posts, Indian villages. Even by his enemies he is known for fairness, kindness and, just like you, generosity."

Standing together in front of the hearth, he rocked her gently in his arms as the fire eased down its heat.

Webster spoke in a near whisper. "A man like that doesn't rape someone. Although he never married, when Blue Stone thought he was about to die, he gave all his worldly goods to Medicine Bear. Miraculously, he didn't die and refused to take back anything that he had given away."

Georgia looked up. "Is he still alive?"

"That's who I am going to meet at the Sun Dance and ... I thought if you met him ... I have to say this before I lose my courage ... I was hoping you would marry me there during the ceremony."

"Yes! Yes! To everything, yes!"

Full of spontaneity and full to the brim with love, their lips melded and molded perfectly together. All semblance of physical barriers disappeared. Souls merged though bodies were kept modest and warm.

She hung the dress so she could see it full length beside the fireplace and admired it every day.

Topics of conversation over the days leading to the Sun Dance were centered on hopes and desires. Webster was able to show her how to depend upon and be grateful for God's guidance. He told a story of being near death in the desert with no water for over a week. He lay on the sand, so weak he couldn't stand, and prayed for rain. In less than an hour, it rained. Georgia smiled, "Sounds like the time I was starving in the winter of 1848," she teased.

"There are times when I feel like there is nothing solid beneath me at all. I am completely severed, my feet don't touch anything solid, and I'm fully awake."

Webster went on. "Those are times I'm living completely by the grace of God, but not wanting or hoping for anything—just open and ready for His will to move me. When I come upon travelers in need of help, or a ranch short of hands, I help until it is clear I'm no longer needed."

Georgia listened intently to his stories and took them all to heart.

"When some Indians do a vision quest, they take no food or water with them. Some don't even take a knife or flint to make a fire. They go nearly naked, with no blankets or hides. That puts them completely in the hands of the Creator. I've tried to live that way."

"What do you say about all that has happened to me? What has God had to do with that? I'm ready to forget all the anger and hatred I've held over the years, but I still don't understand what on earth God had in mind when all the death and pain rained down in my life, flooding out all goodness."

"You must find those answers for yourself. It's not for me to do. That's all between you and God. Ask Him for understanding and be patient for the answer. It will come."

The last three words had a strange feel to them. They both felt it. A finality that resembled the closing of a large book from the middle—weighty pages slapping together with a thump.

Many people of Blue Stone's tribe had become sick with the smallpox. A few survived and Medicine Bear had found the source and burned all the blankets. However, Blue Stone had a slight case and because of his age made him weak and less able to overcome it. He lay for days with raging fevers and ranted deliriously.

Plans for the Sun Dance were halted and no one wanted to celebrate it if Blue Stone was not going to lead it.

Medicine Bear sent Jumping Fox, one of the braves who had been hunting game with Webster because he knew where he stayed. The young brave rode off at a full gallop. Medicine Bear was hoping Webster would bring Georgia quickly. With good weather, and no other incidents it would take him a week to get to Webster. Jumping

Fox was to marry the woman the dress was made for.

The girl had shown him the dress when it was nearly finished and her mother had kept it after the girl died.

The Sun Dance was weeks away. Georgia went to the town of Benton to find a sachet or some perfume, whatever she could afford to enhance her wedding wardrobe with the aroma of flowers. Women in the town stared at her, with her boots, hat and buckskins. She only wore them now on long rides, but they molded to her like butter and she reveled in the chance to don them. She stared back at the women wearing fancy hats with netting and lace. The shoes that took a long time to button were the oddest thing to her eyes.

While Georgia was in Benton, Webster was roaming the fields, looking for stray calves, when he saw Jumping Fox riding toward him at a full gallop. Webster invited him into the house for some food and drink and when the Indian boy saw the dress he couldn't believe his eyes. He said nothing and Webster left the boy to finish his food, while he rushed off to find Georgia.

The dress was precious to him for the memory of his loved one and he took it to keep it near, something of her to hold, when he rode back to the tribe. Taking precious things or items needed for survival was not thought of as 'stealing,' but a matter of course in native custom. It was seen more as an insult to the loser of the item than a shame to the taker.

Georgia's ride back to the ranch should have only taken two days and nights, but she stretched it another day. The weight of the step she was about to take and the prospect of facing the unknown with another human being awakened doubts. She had to do something she was sure of and followed the tracks of a mountain lion until they vanished near a rocky outcropping. Way up among the disheveled boulders, the beautiful cat rested, looking out over its domain from its perfect vantage point, watching for food or for threats in the distance.

The jawline is not as pronounced as a male. Must be a female. Georgia smiled and turned the horse toward the ranch. The cat watched her until she was completely out of sight.

One more night she stayed 'in the wild', far from the sight of ranches' lanterns or the sound of reins jingling and wagons rattling over rutted roads in the distance. A few stars braved the upper atmosphere and gave their last light. *For my eyes only,* she told herself.

A meager meal of a biscuit and a cup of buffalo broth served as a fast. In town she'd denied her body what it had been demanding: a huge steak and a healthy mound of potatoes baptized in freshly churned butter. This was the closest she could come to fasting for a vision quest. The time was perfect.

"God. I come to You humbly, hungry, and with what semblance of reverence I can muster. I believe You will answer. Webster convinced me You have had my interest in Your heart and in Your care. Please, show me what You want for me, so I will have no doubt."

She waited in silence and tried to clear her mind of all thought, as Webster had tried to teach her.

The brush around her rustled as a breeze moved in a wide circle. It didn't touch her fire or raise any dirt and sand. It surrounded her gently, enclosed her with invisible arms, but didn't touch her. The breeze continued to whisper through the brush—at the same distance—rising and falling in hushed tones like a lullaby created by wings of angels, until she fell asleep.

Replays of the disparaging looks from the town women appeared just before her dream. And when they were gone, a point of light captured her attention. The light was the size of a single pea and appeared to be an arm's length away. She reached out to touch it. It moved exactly the length of her reach. She 'moved' toward it. It moved exactly the distance she had advanced.

Well, that's frustrating.

In her dream state she turned away, but a curtain of light was spread before her instead. Webster stepped out from within it. In an instant she understood everything that had happened in her life—*before* and *after* she and Webster had found each other. Her heritage, his philosophy, their love, wouldn't be what they were if everything that had happened to each of them were any different.

She woke to the melodies of the cactus wren cheering the sun up.

Twenty-Three

All My Relations (Indians use this word instead of relatives)

Footsteps padded behind her when she began to pack up. She was aware of them but not wary. The assurance of lifelong protection had finally been absorbed by her psyche. Ready to respond with quick moves she continued to move about her campsite with confidence.

Suddenly, she was encircled with a pair of arms, and a familiar voice whispered in her ear, "So you thought you could get away." A two-day growth of beard stubble brushed her cheek.

In a flash, she turned and her arms encircled his neck.

"How did you find me?" she breathed.

"I got on ol' Rambler, it was like there was a magnet in my gut that pulled me straight to you."

It occurred to her what a gift this was from the unseen force in their lives. A divine gift tailored in every detail just for the two of them. It had all the elements that fit them. Then he said, "Something has happened. Blue Stone."

"What? "she said, then held her breath waiting the answer.

"He is very sick, the Sun Dance is postponed, but "we must go now," he said.

In all their time and talks he had never told her of his promise to Blue Stone, but now was the perfect time.

"Many years ago, Blue Stone asked me to find his daughter by a white woman. I promised and left my family shortly after my mother died to fulfill that promise. It was the most difficult thing I ever had to do up to that point in my life." She listened with complete attention. He continued, "I found your mother and baby brother at the farm and I buried them, then I searched for you for years until I felt it was time to report to Blue Stone that I had not found you."

Tears streamed down her face and to her neck.

"I spent years with the tribe until the war broke out and he bade me well and released me from my promise to see to my people. I built and repaired wagons for the army and for civilian use and after the war, began my search for you again."

"After so much 'trying' to find you—I stopped 'trying' and let God lead me to you. That took only a brief time, I don't know how long, but it was a lot shorter than the years I spent."

Georgia felt weak and sat hard on the ground.

"You mean he wanted me and looked for me after mother died." She asked.

"He said Julia came to him in a dream and told him you were alone and asked him to protect you. He knew after the dream that she was dead. He told me he sent braves to watch you and they lost you when you crossed the Mississippi."

Thinking back, there were times she saw a few braves passing in a distance, and the group that showed her how to get out of the mud by charging through the forest, and maybe even the old man on the barge.

"Do you think we can get there in time? Let's not waste another minute. Lead the way—OH NO!" she shrieked, "I don't have my dress. That beautiful dress! I must have my dress. It would mean so much to him and to me."

Webster was so stunned at those words it threw him off balance to the point he tilted off his saddle. The concept of Georgia wanting a dress badly enough to change directions would have been unthinkable for most of her life. He was aware of that. He also had no idea how to solve the problem.

It should have been an easy choice, who wouldn't choose family over a dress? But the dress was so much more. Acceptance of her heritage and proof to her father that she could love him and his people were layered and intricately sewn into her spirit and the best way to show it was to wear the dress that said it all.

"Whatever you choose will be a fateful decision, " he said, "because of what is at stake either way you decide."

She felt it too, the draw of the power of sacrifice and the critical aspect to 'do the right thing' in this moment.

Her mind weighed all the pieces she was aware of and when she thought of leaving the dress, her heart felt at peace.

"Let's go!" Off they rode side by side until dark.

Jumping Fox rode like the wind with the dress wrapped again in the winter coat of his namesake, tucked tightly under the blanket between him and his horse's back. He remembered his intended bride's laugh and their sweet moments together. He had been away when she died from a strange fever. He grieved because he did not get to say the kind of good bye that would release him from his pangs of guilt.

Throughout the nights of their travel, Webster and Georgia were mostly silent, so comfortable within themselves, and between the two of them, speaking was unnecessary. They enjoyed the same things: being in the outdoors, sitting by a campfire, listening to songs nature provided, and looking into each other's eyes.

A wolf pack ran parallel to Jumping Fox and gathered near his camp whenever he stopped to rest.

Medicine Bear could talk to animals and understood when they talked back in their own language. He had sent the wolves to follow the young brave, and a hawk to follow Georgia and Webster. The hawk returned to Medicine Bear each day to report the traveler's progress. The wolves were to protect their human from other predators.

Finally, after so many days of being obedient to the promise made to Medicine Bear, the lure of the fox skin overcame their restraint. The lead wolf snatched the package away, from the brave's camp the last night of travel and ran into the forest with it. The young man was sleeping and didn't discover it until morning. He thought some spirit had come and taken it and rode home disheartened.

The wolves inspected the package thoroughly and deftly removed the fox wrapping. Each one had to taste with their snout, paw at the hide, and take turns in order of their rank to explore the doeskin dress. There was much yelping and growling and fur flying as the challenges for higher rank were being made. The dress lay flat out in their midst, but was untouched.

During their rides together, Webster frequently rode ahead at a gallop to send wildlife scattering or chasing off threats—like wolves. Then he doubled back to ride with Georgia. He could see these wolves' faces darting behind the shrubs with toothy mouths as they vied for position. He had no idea what the fuss was about, but to be safe he rode in their direction to move them off further away from human life. They left their prize on the forest floor. A pup had yanked off a single fringe, the rest was undamaged, but laying almost full length so it could not be missed or mistaken for anything other than what it was.

Even though many times such coincidences had occurred in his life, each one was as astonishing as the first. He dismounted and approached the dress in disbelief. Fearing it might disappear when he got closer; he held his breath and tiptoed up to it. When his fingers stroked the fringes the dress stayed visible and he exhaled. Gathering it up, and tucking it back into the fox fur he started singing Oh! Susannah while riding back to show Georgia the miracle.

He had said they were only a day from the camp. While he was gone, Georgia washed her hair with soap plant, crushed rose petals and rubbed the liquid into her skin.

She put off donning the buckskins as long as she could, but the morning chill stung like nettles and she slipped into them with resignation. She had never put the dress on, waiting for The Day, so it would be as fresh as it could be. Now she tried to imagine putting it on and stroking the softness and combing the fringes straight and true. With her eyes closed she petted the air where fringes might hang. Webster could be heard a long way off on his galloping horse and singing at the top of his lungs.

The back hooves of the horse dug deep into the ground when Webster pulled up the reins, jumped off, and tossed the package right into her arms. When his feet hit the ground, he grabbed her and spun her around in the air.

None of it registered with her for a while, the thought of him having the dress was unimaginable. But when he finally put her down and she could see for herself it really was the dress. Shock, to the point of numbness, was the only thing she could feel. Then overwhelming joy. Pulling off the buckskins, and slipping into the dress happened so quickly, Webster merely blinked and the change of clothes was complete.

Blue Stone had gotten well during their ride to his side. His greatest improvement came when he heard she was coming.

Georgia rode side saddle most of the way to the ceremony. A half mile away, Webster walked his horse and they came into view side by side. The camp was in a clearing near a forest of lodge pole pine, the trees used to make the frame of the Sun Dance structure. The frame stood bare boned because that was as far as the preparations had gotten when Blue Stone became ill.

She and Webster entered the gathering where dozens of teepees were standing in semi-circle formation, her hair, with its bright contrasting streak, was wavy from having braided it tightly when wet and lay like a silvery shawl arcing over her back and shoulders.

No other dress was as beautifully decorated. It's weight kept her posture from being haughty, but her back was straight and she held her head with dignity, not pride. The third generation Moonshine's coat gleamed in the sun as he carried her to the center of the village. She slid down his side and the cry of a hawk came from above. Medicine Bear had called it home and it began to dive fiercely at her head. She wrapped the reins around her wrist and thrust her arm to the sky. The bird landed easily and folded its wings.

Without missing a step, she kept walking to the revered elder of this tribe, with her eyes looking straight ahead.

Each footstep bringing her closer to the object of her life-long hatred, every footstep matching the beat of the drum, every beat of the drum scattering a bit of bitterness and replacing it with humility. Blue Stone, stood with his arms open wide, waiting to meet the daughter he had sent braves to protect, made sacrifices and fasted to ask The Spirits to keep her safe. The daughter born by the woman whose only language they shared was one of transcendent love.

Georgia saw the tears in his eyes and knew he must have truly loved Julia because she could feel his love for herself.

Raising her arm quickly she released Harley and he circled above her.

She stepped into Blue Stone's arms and he enfolded her until she disappeared completely in his embrace. Now there was no doubt. She lay her head on his chest. Her own heart was beating as it did the first time her hawk came to rest on her arm, the drumbeat inside his chest matched that of the sacred drum uniting all who could hear it. When father and daughters beats matched, she whispered, "Father." And he whispered, "Falling Star."

After the ceremony of the Sun Dance, Webster and Georgia were married by Blue Stone in the Indian way by entering a teepee Blue Stone's niece had prepared for them. They stayed in the camp until the fall then left for New Mexico. Blue Stone gave her the piece of turquoise mysteriously in tact. He told Webster the truth of the stone before the couple rode away to begin their life.

Many years of hard work and happiness followed.

One early evening when the sky was painted with rich oranges and royal purple she went out to the porch to admire it and found Webster in the matching rocker. The pallor and peace on his face was unmistakable. The colors of the sky were much the same as those the night he leaned over her shoulder and said ,"God is painting the skies and sending His love to you." At this moment those colors were reflected in the canvas of his white mane and beard.

The picture it made was so lovely, she stood looking at it, memorizing every shade, and nuance before kissing his cheek. Their life had been so thoroughly satisfying; there was nothing she would miss. He would be a part of her always. She touched him tenderly and with only her thoughts said, "Go with God, my love." Knowing he would hear.

He was buried on November 11th and she stood by his grave until the stars began to fall.

Twenty-Four

October 20, 2014

Adrienne sighed as she collected her purse, her folders, the mail and a Kleenex from the front seat then sat staring out the windshield, dreading another hum-drum night to refresh for another hum-drum day. The shrubs beside the driveway hid her front door from view and she nearly dropped everything in her arms when she saw the old trunk sitting there.

"What on earth?"

Sweetums, her cat, sitting in the window, was stretching his neck and bobbing his head, trying to see what that strange box was on his porch, too.

Adrienne hurried into the house, dropped off the bundle in her arms, and rushed back out to inspect the mysterious trunk. She quickly discovered she couldn't lift it alone and went to Tom, the retired professor next door, for help.

He was stout enough that he might have been able to drag it by himself, but the two of them worked together to carry it into the garage.

"Missy, what *is* this? Where'd it come from?" Tom was as excited about it as she was.

"I don't know. I haven't found any identifying information on it yet."

They both walked around and around it.

"Here it is!" Tom said. "It's from something, something, Dunbar in Midlothian, Illinois."

"It must have cost a fortune to send it all the way out here to Utah." Adrienne said.

"Look at that lock!" Tom said. "You don't see them like that anymore. It's as much an antique as the trunk. This thing must be full of real antiques of some kind." Tom patted the big box as he spoke.

"You get to open it," Adrienne added, "I think you have the skills to unlock it without damaging anything. If I were to do it, I'd take a hammer to it just to get the job done in a hurry."

"Really! When can I start?"

"Now, if you want. I'll make us some tea while you get your tools."

Adrienne Michaels tried to remember who in the world still lived in Illinois that was named Dunbar. No friend or family member came to mind.

She had to look up the family tree that her niece had given her a few Christmases ago to find the Dunbar branch.

There it was, dating back to the 1800s: Phineas married Julia, who had Sean. Only Phineas' brothers and Julia's sisters were recorded with them. Sean died at the age of four, and there was no information on Savannah, at all. No children, no husband, nothing.

"I'm back!" Tom called out from the garage.

The treasure within would soon be exposed.

Tom straightened up to stretch the knot out of his back before breaking the lock and looked at Adrienne, who stood a few feet away holding her breath.

Click, thump. The lock fell open.

Adrienne lifted the lid and the stale air from the aging papers, photos, and undiscovered objects swept over her torso, up past her nostrils, eyes, and hair. She closed her eyes as the gust drenched her body like a baptism from the ages. The embrace of a wild spirit kept in this dark prison for almost one hundred years pressed against her briefly and left its nostalgic perfume hanging in the air.

A lace curtain with a note attached—*To Georgia from Mrs. McDaniels*—covered a doeskin dress with beautiful beading and fringes. Beneath the dress, enfolded by it, lay volumes of diaries. On top of the diaries was an envelope. Adrienne opened it and read the letter written in very fine handwriting.

'To Savannah Georgia Dunbar-Michaels' relatives. These remembrances have been handed down and protected by her Aunt Clara, her friend Ebony Rose, and her cousins—the Dunbars and Michaels, to you. In these diaries you

will find her stories and events that you may think are fiction. They are, for the most part, true. Her wedding dress and how she came to own it is found in them. Pass them on.'

At the very bottom of the trunk, nestled in a handmade wooden box, was the largest piece of turquoise Adrienne had ever seen.

"What's this?"

That's another story.

END

www.ingramcontent.com/pod-product-compliance
Lightning Source LLC
Chambersburg PA
CBHW032014170626
46807CB00006B/2801